For first news of
titles, give-aways and
discounts, sign up to our
infrequent newsletter at:
oleanderpress.com

MURDER
AT THE
COLLEGE

VICTOR L. WHITECHURCH

This edition published 2022 by
The Oleander Press
16 Orchard Street
Cambridge
CB1 1JT

Murder at the College was originally published in 1932

Cataloguing in Publication Data
A catalogue record for this book is available
from the British Library

ISBN 9781999900489

Front cover image © Mary Evans Picture Library
Typesetting and eBook by neorelix

FOREWORD

IT is, perhaps, unfortunate that the "Detective Story" is so often confused with the "Thriller," for it does not at all follow that they are one and the same thing. A "Thriller" by its very name, is a story full of exciting incidents. It may, in a sense, be a "Detective Story" in that it often deals with the elucidation of a crime. But in the elucidation of that particular crime other crimes, hair-breadth escapes, terrible "situations" follow – to make up a succession of "thrills" for the reader.

Now, in ordinary life, it is not usual for detectives to be faced with a constant succession of "thrills" in the course of tracking down a crime. In a murder case, for example, one will rarely find three or four further murders connected with the case under investigation. And, to produce a genuine "Detective Story" which has for its purpose the presentation of facts rather than imagination, such "thrills" should be avoided. The true "Detective Story" is a "problem," the problem of how some particular crime was committed and who committed it, a problem which, while often demanding smaller problems, should not deviate from the main question in hand. "A Crime, and its solution." That is the description of the real "Detective Story."

In the pages which follow, this description has been strictly adhered to. The problem is gradually worked out on the ordinary lines of shrewd police investigation and methods. Every detail of the investigation, as it arises, is made plain to the reader – as he reads, he knows just as much about the case as the detective knows – no less. The author has tried to "play the game" fairly, and, in order to do so, he has strictly avoided "thrills."

VICTOR L. WHITECHURCH.

I

"HALLO! There he is again. First Tuesday in the month, as per usual."

"Who?"

"That chap getting out of his four-seater at the college gateway opposite. You watch him. He'll bring out his luggage now. Ah; what did I tell you? Two suitcases and a big brown-paper roll. Always the same. Now I wonder what he's got in that roll. Big as a couple of small drain pipes set end to end, eh? I get to fancying all sorts of things about that luggage. Tell you what, Budgen, I ought to have been a detective instead of sweating out my guts in an insurance office. I've got the sense of curiosity pretty strongly and there isn't much chance of satisfying it in keeping a ledger and filling in policies. Now, that fellow opposite – "

"Who is he?"

"Hanged if I know; but, as I say, I'm curious. There he goes. The porter's carried in his goods and he's off to garage his car. He'll be there again just before eleven – with the rest of 'em. Now, who *are* they? And why the dickens do they meet over there once a month? I *would* like to know. See that bow window?"

And he pointed across the street to an oriel window on the first floor of St. Oswald's College over the way.

"Well?"

"That's the room where they meet. And, whatever their business is, they're at it all day – except when they pop out to lunch. About a dozen of 'em, there are. You'll see them come along presently. . . . Best get on with those letters now. The boss will be asking for them in a jiffy."

And he glanced at the office clock. Budgen's typewriter began to click, and George Wilkins, senior clerk in the Exbridge branch of the United Assurance Company, Limited, bending over his desk by the window, applied himself to sundry columns of figures.

These offices of the company were situated on the second floor over a tailor's and outfitter's shop in the High Street of the university city of Exbridge, opposite St. Oswald's College, and the particular room in which Wilkins and the new junior clerk worked looked out on the street. The temptation, therefore, to glance from time to time at that busy thoroughfare was irresistible to one who numbered a sense of curiosity among his other accomplishments.

"Hallo!" he exclaimed presently. "They're beginning to come along – in twos and threes as usual. Look! There's the fellow who drove up in the car just now – I call him the President – and two parsons with him. The tall one who looks as though he'd crack if he bent is the Reverend

Starchey, and the little chap with the broad grin on his face the Reverend Smiley."

"How do you know their names?"

"I don't. I call 'em what they look like. Here come two more – the Colonel, that's the big chap with the moustache. And the clean-shaven fellow with a flower in his buttonhole looks a regular nob, eh? I've put him down as the Duke – and there's the Little Joker."

"Which one?"

"Chap in plus fours with a beard. Lively little beggar. Always seems to be making funny remarks to the others. Look at him now! Old Sir Lanky Walrus – that thin fellow with the drooping moustache – is laughing at something he's told him. Now, notice that blighter, just come up, in the light-grey suit and the white tie. I can't quite place him, but I'm nearly certain he's another parson. I've dubbed him the Waiter out for a spree. Looks it, don't he? I wonder what they do over the way. They've all got dispatch cases."

"Lecturers or something of that sort, very likely."

"Not they! It's out of term time just now, so that can't be it. For the same reason they can't be examiners – "

He stopped short. The door opened and the branch manager came in, putting an end to further conversation or surmises.

Oblivious of the fact that they were being closely scrutinised, the objects of George Wilkins's curiosity passed, in their twos or threes, through the portal of St. Oswald's College, the porter, who was standing at the entrance, saluting them respectfully as they entered. He also had a word of warning to give them.

"Take care," he said, "when you get to the foot of Mr. Henlow's staircase. They're doing something to the drainage, and there's a big hole there."

Passing through the gateway they found themselves in a beautiful, grass-spread quad, surrounded by the grey walls of the ancient college. They turned sharply to the right, and, when they reached the corner, to the left, pacing the stone walk bordering the grass. About two-thirds of the way along this walk, they turned again to the right through an archway into a small inner quad – a region of supreme silence, for here the traffic of the street was completely hushed.

Ignoring the path to the left, which led into another part of the college, again they turned right, and, in the extreme corner of the quad, found a doorless entrance. At this entrance they realised the porter's warning. Two men were at work there. They had removed several of the flagstones and had excavated quite a large hole. The piled-up earth lay on one side of the doorway, and, over the cavity, they had placed a couple of boards to form a rough bridge. These two men stood, tools in hand, while the various members of the little company passed over the temporary bridge.

"Sorry to trouble you," said one of them civilly; "but we shall have finished the job before the day's over, and put it all straight again."

"Oh, that's all right," replied the "President" stepping carefully over the boards; "we shan't disturb you for a couple of hours. But we shall be coming out to lunch at about one o'clock – till half-past two."

"Glad you told me that, sir," answered the workman. "My mate and I will be off for our dinner at one, and we shan't have filled in this hole by then. So we'll have these boards across again, ready for you."

Immediately inside the doorway were two small flights of well-worn, oaken stairs emerging above into a very short landing with a door on either side of it. The door on the left had nothing to mark it, but that on the right bore an ancient visiting card, fixed to it with a couple of drawing pins, and bearing, engraved upon it, the name, "Mr. Sidney Henlow."

The "President," who was the first to ascend the stairs, opened this door, without knocking and, followed by the others as they arrived singly or in twos and threes, entered a good-sized room. On the left was a window looking into the small quad, on the right two windows, one of them an oriel, overlooking the street. A long, broad table stood in the middle of the room, the fireplace was between the two windows, and flanked by a couple of low capacious armchairs. Ordinary chairs were ranged round the table. On the wall opposite the door was a bookcase, stretching across the room from the oriel window, but not all the way across; the remaining space being occupied by a door which evidently opened into an inner apartment. A low, cushioned seat was arranged round the half-circle of the oriel window. Such was the room of Mr. Sidney Henlow. And Mr. Sidney Henlow himself was a fellow of St. Oswald's College, an eminent classical scholar, and a lecturer on Greek literature. The above named bookcase carried more than one volume with his name on the title page.

When all were duly gathered together the "Reverend Starchey" took his place at the head of the table, and the others seated themselves thereat. The "President," who was, as a matter of fact the secretary, removed from the suitcases formidable bundles of documents and from the brown paper equally formidable looking rolls, and they began their work for the day.

Who were they? Well, in the first place, every man among them, clerical or lay, was a person of sound judgment and knowledge, and refinement. They were united in the common bond of excellent taste and artistic outlook, and several of the laymen were entitled to write the letters F.S.A., or R.A., after their names. The "President" was Mr. Stacey Pennington, high in his profession as an architect; "Starchey" was that artistically gifted cleric, Canon Alan Rushmere; the "Colonel" was Sir John Littleport, not a professional, but an acknowledged connoisseur in the art world; the "Duke" was Francis Hatton, a dilettante country gentleman with a profound knowledge of architecture; the "Little Joker," an artist named Stanhope, an absolute enthusiast, was one of the best-known authorities on Mediaeval Ecclesiastical Art in the country; "Sir Lanky Walrus" was Guy Buckland, a prominent architect; the parson who had been dubbed the "Waiter out on a spree," possessed a judgment on the decoration of churches which was second to none. His real name was James Kershaw. Besides these, there were Canon Herbert Finstock, Angus

McPhail, Hartley Prior, and the individual whose name appeared on the card outside the door – Sidney Henlow, every one of whom was, in some way or other, conversant with art in its best sense.

These men had been appointed by the Bishop of Exbridge to form a committee upon which each served without payment or reward, and rejoiced in serving – the "Consultative Committee," for so it was called. This committee exercised an important function in the Diocese of Exbridge. Nothing was allowed to be done in churches in the way of alterations, memorials, windows and so forth, without reference being made to it and its expert advice being bestowed. The diocese was a large one, and every month brought an accumulation of work. Installation of electric light or heating apparatus, new furniture, altars, choir stalls, screens, tablets and other memorials, enlargements of buildings, organs – there was an infinite variety. The chancellor of the diocese would rarely issue the necessary faculty for work to be done without the approval of the Consultative Committee. Many parishes submitted their schemes to the committee before attempting to approach the chancellor for a faculty. And the committee, on these Tuesdays, carefully and deliberately examined every case brought before it, read descriptive letters, studied plans and specifications, and approved or turned down or suggested alterations as the case might be.

They were all experts and they were all friends. Their meetings though conducted on business lines, had an informal air about them, nevertheless. Most of them smoked, and they approved or criticized freely, but rarely failed to be unanimous in their decision. They were a gathering of brothers in art. They could have met, like other diocesan committees, at the formal, barely furnished diocesan offices in the city, but Henlow had placed his rooms in St. Oswald's College at their disposal. They met, therefore, comfortably and in happy surroundings. They lunched in little companionable groups at their favourite restaurants, and Henlow always gave them tea before they broke up. They got through a great deal of work on those Tuesdays, but it was all attractive and congenial work, and they, really, thoroughly enjoyed the day. For they were an extremely pleasant little coterie.

So, whatever speculations the young insurance clerk opposite had, from time to time, as to who they were and what they did, the facts are now clear and above board. They were a committee of experts, "consultative," as to their title, but their advice in nine cases out of ten took the form of "injunctions." They had considerable power, and parishes which came forward with impracticable or inartistic schemes for church restoration or other like matters, knew it!

At eleven o'clock on this first Tuesday in September nine of the committee turned up for their day's work. Pennington produced, from his brown-paper roll, sundry plans and drawings and opened his suitcases, which were filled with more plans, specifications and correspondence. Canon Rushmere took the chair and several of the members lighted pipes. They were friendly and informal in their methods. Before reading the minutes of the last meeting Pennington produced a post card.

"This is from Henlow," he said; "I received it last Friday – posted, apparently, at Geneva. I'll read it."

It was only a few lines, as follows:

"Sorry I shall not be present at the Consultative Committee next Tuesday, but I've instructed Williams to have my room ready as usual for you, and to provide tea.

Yours, SIDNEY HENLOW."

Williams, one of the college servants, had evidently received Henlow's instructions, for a cheerful fire was burning in the grate, and, in the course of the morning, Williams himself came in and asked for how many he should prepare tea. Seven decided to stay. Hatton said he wanted to leave early, and Sir John Littleport was going to drink tea with a don of his acquaintance – at another college.

Patiently and deliberately they began discussing, one by one, the long list of proposals and applications on their programme. Several members reported visits they had paid to sundry churches since the last meeting. That was another item in their work. They came from various parts of the large diocese, most of them possessed cars, and in cases of difficulty or those in which personal inspection of some proposed work in a church was advisable, it was their custom to ask those who lived in the various districts to run out, see things for themselves and report.

"Now," said Pennington presently, reaching for a new bundle of correspondence, "we've got a bit of a difficulty here – Little Marpleton Church again."

"What, that window?" asked Buckland.

"Exactly."

"But I thought we'd settled that? Turned it down, didn't we?"

"Not quite," said Canon Rushmere; "you may remember we suggested some drastic changes in the design, and advised the chancellor accordingly. It's a chancellor's case. They applied to him for the faculty without consulting us first, and he sent everything on to us."

"And are they willing to make our suggested alterations?" asked Hartley Prior.

"Well," replied the secretary, "Hatton will give us information about that. You went over to Little Marpleton, didn't you, Hatton?"

Hatton took his pipe from his mouth and laughed.

"I did," he said, "and it wasn't altogether a pleasant visit."

"Tell us about it," said the chairman.

"Well," said Hatton, "the trouble is that in the parish there's a squire of the old-fashioned sort – old Matthew Finmere. He hasn't imbibed any twentieth-century notions, and he wants to rule the village – parson, church and all – with a rod of iron. And he's able to do so, to a large extent. Most of the folks there are his tenants, and he's the patron of the living. He is a crusty old fellow, with a violent temper, and as stingy as you can make 'em, though he has plenty of money. A year ago his wife died – poor woman, I fancy he gave her rather a time of it! Whether from compunction of the way he treated her or whether we allow that he had some affection for her, he wants to hand down her memory to posterity by putting in a coloured window, in place of the plain glass at the east end of the chancel, and, incidentally, to glorify himself by a preposterous inscription on a huge brass under the window-sill, just above the altar.

"Without consulting anyone, he went to a fellow who calls himself an artist. Finmere himself, I must tell you, has no more taste than that which enables him to judge a bit of horseflesh or to give you the vintage of a glass of port. He knows nothing whatever about art. Well, he got this chap – Hastings is his name – "

"Hastings?" broke in Stanhope. "I know the beast." Stanhope was always violent in his expressions. "A fourth-rate dauber in crude colours – designs all out of drawing – I wouldn't employ him to put a window in a pig-sty – turn any respectable pig into one of the Gadarene swine. Go on, Hatton."

"Well, this fellow Hastings submitted a design, and old Finmere said it was just what he wanted."

"He *would*," growled Stanhope.

"Then he got the vicar to call a meeting of the Parochial Church Council. Finmere's a churchwarden, so of course he's on the council. In fact, he is the council to all intents and purposes. The vicar mildly suggested that the whole thing was inappropriate, and drew a storm on his head –

poor chap. They passed a unanimous resolution to apply for the faculty to put the window in. And that's that."

"Well, I went there last week and met the vicar, and the squire in the church. The vicar didn't say much – couldn't; but old Finmere went for me hammer and tongs. I tried to make him see reason and to persuade him to go to an artist who would design something worthy of the church – and the tracery of the window, which is a beautiful perpendicular one. But he wouldn't hear anything. He said he'd given Hastings the order and that the window was being made, and added he didn't intend to throw away his money for the sake of a parcel of damned interfering idiots."

"Meaning us?" said Canon Rushmere.

"Meaning us. And he went on to say that he meant to put the window in, faculty or no faculty."

"He can't do that, of course," said Littleport. "Let's have another look at the design."

Whereupon Pennington unrolled a huge design and affixed it, with drawing pins, to the bookcase. The others rose from their seats and spread around it in a semi-circle. It was, certainly, a perfectly hideous design, crude both in drawing and colouring. It represented St. Cecilia (the late Mrs. Finmere was something of a pianist, and had played the organ in the church) clad in green and yellow, holding an impossible harp, and surrounded by admiring, longhaired, anaemic-looking angels, with rainbow wings and gaudy robes.

"Oh!" exclaimed Stanhope; "preposterous – terrible! It mustn't be allowed, of course. It won't do at all."

There was a general consensus of the same opinion, and the secretary was instructed to return the design to the chancellor with every expression of disapproval, and to advise him not to issue the faculty. The committee proceeded to discuss other business.

It was about ten minutes to one that they agreed, after carefully consulting the plans, on the erection of a new reredos in Catfield Church. The secretary glanced at the agenda.

"The next case," he said, "is rather a complicated one. It concerns the removal of the organ in Westinghurst Church from its present position in the ancient chapel beside the chancel. They want to rebuild it at the west end of the church, and restore the chapel. I think we'd better adjourn it till after luncheon."

This was agreed upon. Members of the committee began putting on overcoats and hats, and departed in twos or threes to restaurants. Hatton was still seated at the table. Stanhope was lighting his pipe. All the others had gone. He turned to Hatton.

"I'm going to feed at the Bell," he said, naming a restaurant. "Coming with me, Hatton?"

"No," replied Hatton; "I've brought my luncheon with me and I'm going to have it here. I've – er – a letter or two to write."

"All right," said Stanhope, who had come back to the table. "Hallo! I hadn't noticed this."

And he took up a book.

"What is it?"

"Oh, the report of the Society for the Preservation of Ancient Monuments. I expect Henlow left it out for us to look at. I wonder what it says about that old market cross at Frattenbury." He was consulting the index. "Er – page fifty-two – it isn't cut."

Hatton pushed across the table a paper-cutter, or what served Henlow as such. In reality it was a small dagger, with heavy, bronze handle, and blade of about six inches in length. Stanhope picked it up and cut a leaf of the book.

"Ah – not very much, I see. By George, Hatton, that's quite a dangerous-looking weapon." And he laid the paper-knife down on the table. "Well, if you won't come, I'll be off. See you again at half-past two."

Hatton nodded. He had taken a paper from his pocket and was looking at it. Stanhope went out of the room, glancing at his wrist-watch as he did so. Three minutes to one!

II

THE first members of the Consultative Committee who returned to St. Oswald's College after their luncheon were Julian Stanhope, the little, bearded artist, and the Reverend James Kershaw, the parson of the grey suit and white tie. George Wilkins, the allotted hour for his midday meal having passed, had just come into his office, and glancing through the window saw the two men apparently on the point of entering the college opposite, saw them go through the gateway, and thereupon riveted his attention on a fresh column of figures.

Meanwhile, Stanhope and Kershaw, discussing a point that had been raised in the morning, walked partly round the first quad, passed through the archway to the inner one, turned sharply to the right and reached the open entrance to the stairway. There they paused for just a moment – Stanhope wanted to light his pipe. The two workmen were at the entrance of the staircase, one of them standing in the hole that had been excavated.

"Half a moment," he said, looking up as the two men stood there. "I'll put the boards across for you to get over – beg pardon, sir," he went on, speaking to Kershaw; "but did either of you gentlemen drop something when you came out this morning?"

"Why do you ask?"

"When we came back from havin' a bit o' dinner just now, I found this here lyin' in the hole. 'Twasn't there when we went away, I know."

He put his hand in his pocket and produced an object, which he held out to them.

"By George," exclaimed Stanhope; "I know what that is – it's Henlow's paper-knife! I was using it to cut a book with just before I came away. And you found it here, you say?"

"Yes, sir," replied the man. "'Twas half under the loose earth at the bottom, there. Unless I'd shovelled out a bit more of it I shouldn't ha' come across the thing, especially as we're fillin' the hole in now."

"That's rather queer," remarked Kershaw, taking the knife from the man and looking at it. "I wonder how it came there. You were using it, you say, Stanhope?"

"Yes. But I certainly didn't bring it away with me," said Stanhope, with a laugh. "I left it lying on the table."

"Anyone else there?"

"Yes. Hatton. He'd brought his lunch with him and was staying to write letters."

"Well, he's probably there now. We'll ask him about it."

The two men mounted the stairs to the landing, Stanhope opened the door of Henlow's room and went in, Kershaw following him.

"Hallo, Hatton," said Stanhope; "we want to know – "

He stopped short. Hatton was seated, leaning back in one of the low, big armchairs by the side of the fireplace, an open newspaper half-covering the upper part of his body.

"Asleep!" said Kershaw, with a laugh. "Here, wake up, Hatton – you lazy beggar!"

And he went forward and slapped him on the shoulder. But Francis Hatton took no notice. Stanhope, with a sharp exclamation, bent over his face.

"What's the matter?"

The door opened and Canon Rushmere, followed by Sir John Littleport, came into the room. Stanhope turned with one of his swift, jerky movements.

"Hatton's fainted, I'm afraid," he said; "we thought he was asleep, but – "

"Fainted!" interrupted Sir John. "What the deuce . . . here, let me have a look at him – he's as white as a sheet."

There was an ominous ring in Sir John's voice which made the others start and glance at each other.

"Unfasten his collar," suggested Stanhope. Sir John nodded. He pulled aside the newspaper and unbuttoned Hatton's waistcoat.

"Good God!" he cried. "What's this?"

For on Hatton's white shirt was a dark crimson stain. Sir John ripped the shirt and undervest open, and laid his hand on Hatton's chest. When he withdrew it, it was stained with blood.

"He's dead!" he exclaimed. "Kershaw! What are you doing with that knife?"

For Kershaw still held in his hand the knife which the workman had given him. For a moment or two there was a strained silence, for Sir John's question had raised a terrible thought – but only for a moment or two.

"Stanhope will tell you," replied Kershaw, very quietly. He understood the significance of the question.

Stanhope briefly explained.

"Surely you never thought –" he began.

"No, no, of course not," broke in Sir John; "though it was only natural to ask – he's been stabbed – look there. We must take steps at once."

"I'll run down and see the porter," said Canon Rushmere.

"Yes, do," said Sir John who, instinctively, seemed to have taken command of the situation. "And, look here, there's a telephone in his lodge. Ring up the police – and we must get a doctor here at once. And, one moment, Canon, tell the porter to lock the gate and not let anyone out of the college till the police come."

"Good!" ejaculated Stanhope; "a very wise proceeding! Terrible, terrible!" he went on, in his quick, jerky manner.

The other members of the committee were now arriving, horror struck as the tragedy dawned upon them. There was no thought of any further business. They stood there, in little groups, waiting. Canon Rushmere returned from the porter's lodge.

"The police will be here directly," he announced. "The porter is locking the gate as you suggested, Sir John, and no one will be allowed out of college just yet."

"And a doctor?" asked Kershaw.

"Yes. The police are seeing to it – they are bringing their divisional surgeon. Ah – here comes someone."

Footsteps were heard outside ascending the staircase. The door opened and a man in the uniform of a Superintendent of Police appeared in the entrance. For a few moments he stood there, quite still. Behind him the little group could see two other men, in plain clothes.

Superintendent Plestow was a fair type of the modern policeman of higher rank. There was no rotundity about his person, indeed, he inclined to slightness. Also, there were no coarser features about a face that, at first sight, struck one as being pleasing and intellectual – and distinctly handsome. Small, fair moustache, broad forehead, delicate eyebrows above a pair of very kindly grey eyes. When he spoke, it was in a soft, cultured voice, but what he said in the first sentence portrayed the alert policeman.

"Which of you gentlemen discovered the body?" he asked.

Stanhope and Kershaw indicated that it was they.

"Tell me, please; has anything been moved or disturbed since?"

"No, I think not," said Kershaw, "except" – pointing to the recumbent form on the chair – "we undid his waistcoat and shirt to see – "

"Exactly," broke in the superintendent, coming forward into the room a little. "I quite understand. But, beyond that?"

"Nothing has been moved."

"He was dead when you found him?"

"As far as we could judge."

"What time was that, please."

"As near as I can remember a few minutes before the half-hour – half-past two."

The superintendent nodded.

"Doctor," he said, turning to one of the two men who had followed him into the room, "will you kindly make your examination? I will wait till you have finished. I shall want all of you gentlemen to remain for a little while," he added.

The doctor, a tall, thin man, crossed the room and bent over Hatton's body. The others stood, silent. The keen eyes of the superintendent looked around the room, and rested for a few moments as they caught sight of the paper-knife, which Kershaw had laid on the table.

Presently the doctor turned, standing erect, a very grave expression on his face. He shook his head.

"There is nothing to be done," he said slowly. "He must have died almost instantaneously. Stabbed in the heart, superintendent, to put it in non-technical language. I should like to make a further examination afterwards, but – just now – " And he shrugged his shoulders.

"How long has he been dead, doctor?" asked the superintendent.

"A very short time. Certainly not an hour."

"Which of you gentlemen saw him last – alive?"

"I did," said Stanhope.

"How long ago?"

"Just before one o'clock."

The superintendent thought for a moment or two and then said:

"Thank you, Doctor Farnborough. I needn't keep you any longer. Now, gentlemen, please, I don't want to trouble you further than I can help – for my sake as well as yours. I shall ask you, sir, and you" – he nodded in turn to Stanhope and Kershaw – "to remain for a short time. Is either of you the occupant of these rooms, by the way?" And he glanced at the door by the bookcase. He knew something of college interiors and guessed accurately that it opened into a bedroom.

Canon Rushmere, as chairman of the committee, took upon himself to reply.

"No," he said, "they belong to Mr. Sidney Henlow, who is abroad at present. Perhaps I should explain to you, superintendent, that we are all members of a committee of the diocese – appointed by the bishop. We meet once a month to transact business, and Mr. Henlow gives us the use of this room."

"Thank you, sir," said Plestow. "And this unfortunate gentleman was a member of your committee?"

"Exactly."

The superintendent turned to Stanhope.

"You say you saw him last? Yes? Were you alone with him?"

"I was."

"How was that?"

Again it was Canon Rushmere who explained.

"We have an interval for luncheon, and generally go to restaurants in the city. All of us had left this room except Mr. Hatton – and Mr. Stanhope."

"I see," said Plestow. "Well, I won't detain you gentlemen any longer, but I must have your names and addresses before you go, please."

They produced visiting cards, and Pennington said:

"Will you allow me to stay to collect my drawings – and specifications?" And he pointed to the array on the table and floor.

"Yes, but please don't touch them just yet, Ambrose." And he turned to the other man who had come in with him. "Take these gentlemen down and tell Constable Ford they can leave the college. And 'phone from the porter's lodge for a photographer, and the ambulance. Good-afternoon, gentlemen. You'll excuse my saying anything further just now. Will you go with the detective-sergeant, please."

Having dismissed all but Stanhope, Kershaw and Pennington, the superintendent turned to the three men inquiringly.

"You will understand," he said, "that in a pressing case like this time is of importance. I want to make a thorough examination here presently, but there are a few questions I must ask you first. You, sir," and he spoke to Stanhope, "say that you were the last of your company to see this poor gentleman alive. Tell me, please, who is he?"

"His name is Hatton – Francis Hatton. He lives – or rather – lived – at Carnford Manor."

"Near Chiltonbury?"

"Yes."

"His profession?"

"Nothing, superintendent. That is to say, he has private means. Really, I suppose you might call him an architect – he is an F.S.A. Very well known in art circles."

"I see. And his relations? We must let them know at once what has happened."

"He was a widower. His sister, unmarried, keeps house for him."

"Is Carnford Manor on the telephone?"

Stanhope was about to answer when Kershaw interrupted.

"I'm motoring home, superintendent," he said, "and my way lies through Chiltonbury. Wouldn't it be better for me to call at Carnford Manor and break this terrible news to Miss Hatton? You see, I know her very well, and she is not very strong – "

"Thank you, sir. That will be the best plan. Please tell her we shall have to take the body to the mortuary here to begin with. The doctor will want to have a further examination. And now," turning again to Stanhope, he went on, "please tell me exactly what happened when you left Mr. Hatton alone in this room." He paused for a moment.

Ambrose, the detective-sergeant, has just come back with the message that he had 'phoned for the photographer. Plestow motioned him to remain. Then Stanhope explained that Hatton had brought his luncheon with him and that he had said he wanted to write some letters. The superintendent glanced quickly round the room. On one of the broad window-sills were three despatch cases – and a couple of overcoats.

"Is one of those cases Mr. Hatton's?"

"Yes," replied Stanhope. "The further one."

"And those overcoats?"

"The grey one is his."

Plestow crossed the room to the window. First he felt in the pockets of the overcoat. Then he opened the despatch case. From it he took out two small packets wrapped in white paper, and a flask. He tore open the packets.

"He hadn't eaten his luncheon, anyhow," he said. "Here are his sandwiches and biscuits, and cheese – and the flask is full. Did he write any letters, I wonder?" He looked on the table. "None here. Well, I'll search his pockets presently. Now, tell me exactly what happened when you came back here. You two" – indicating Stanhope and Kershaw – "came back together. You met no stranger between the college entrance and this room?"

"No," replied Stanhope.

"We met no one," said Kershaw; "but, in the face of what has happened there was rather a singular thing."

"What was that?"

Kershaw told him about the workman and the knife – pointing to the latter as it lay on the table.

"You've handled it, of course?" said Plestow sharply.

"Well, naturally."

"And the workman too! Not much use trying to find finger-prints – though we must have a shot at it. This knife, eh?" He bent over the table, looking at it curiously.

"So that's what he was stabbed with!" exclaimed Pennington.

The superintendent turned on him quickly.

"You've no right to say that, sir. We don't know – yet."

"But – surely – it looks like it?"

"In my trade," said Plestow dryly, "it doesn't do to act upon what a thing looks like at first sight. We have to build up evidence on something more certain. And until the doctor has compared the wound with this knife blade I form no opinion!"

He asked a few more questions, and then told Kershaw and Stanhope they might go.

"You'll be wanted, of course, for the inquest," he said. "I'll see the coroner as soon as possible and let you know when it will take place.

"Now, sir," he went on to Pennington. "I won't delay you. If you will collect all your papers, please... I only wanted to see that nothing was touched without my observing it... You seem to have a large number of plans!"

"We are rather a busy committee," said Pennington, folding up documents and putting them in his cases. "You see – eh? That's queer!"

"What's queer?" asked Plestow.

"There's something missing. Now, that's very odd."

"What is it?"

"Why," said Pennington, "just before we broke up this morning we were deciding about a matter of a stained-glass window. The design – coloured – was a large one, and I had pinned it on to the bookcase so that we could all see it. I can't find it anywhere."

Hastily he looked through all his plans and specifications.

"No," he went on, "it's not here. Now, what can have become of it?"

"A valuable drawing?" asked the superintendent. Pennington laughed slightly.

"Far from it," he replied, "a most obnoxious bit of work. Not at all the thing anyone would covet."

"Was it here when you left?"

"Yes. I saw it, pinned on the bookcase, as I said."

"But you were not the last to leave?"

"No. Mr. Stanhope and Mr. Kershaw were still here."

"You don't think that they – "

"Certainly not," broke in Pennington. "They wouldn't have taken it away. Stanhope was much more likely to tear up the wretched thing. Well, I must leave it as it is, I suppose. You don't want me any more, superintendent?"

"I think you've told me all I want to know for the moment – thanks very much. Ambrose," he went on to the detective-sergeant, "will you help Mr. Pennington? All right, sir – he'll carry these traps down for you and let you out of the college. Come back afterwards, Ambrose."

The superintendent, left to himself, began to make a careful examination. Without touching the body he looked at it from every point of view. He walked round the room and took stock of each of the windows and their outlook, glanced at the various objects on the table, and so forth. In the midst of it footsteps were heard coming up the stairs. Ambrose entered, followed by a photographer, while two other men set down a light ambulance just outside the door, and waited there.

"I want you to make arrangements for interviewing every one within the college," said the superintendent to Ambrose. "I'll have the porter here, to begin with, as soon as all is clear. You might, too, see if you can get anything out of those two workmen at the foot of the stairs. I'll come to you there, when I've finished."

Routine work followed. Photographs of the dead man and of the room were taken. The body was placed on the ambulance, but not before the superintendent had abstracted the contents of Hatton's pockets. At length he was ready for the removal of the body.

"Tell the porter to come to me here," said Plestow as the bearers and the photographer went out.

Left to himself, the superintendent continued his inspection, entering the inner room. Here he found the usual bachelor bedroom furniture. There were no cupboards, but against one of the walls stood a large, mahogany wardrobe. The superintendent opened it and looked at the contents –

clothes hanging up – hats on the top shelf – some pairs of shoes and slippers on the floor.

He satisfied himself that it was impossible for anyone to be hidden in that room, or, if he had been hidden when Stanhope and Kershaw returned, to have escaped. The one window looked out into the quad, and was much too high for anyone to have dropped out of it. And there were no drain pipes or ivy to help in a climb down. Also, in any case, if anyone had succeeded in getting out of that window the two workmen at the entrance to the stairway would have noticed it. By leaning out the superintendent could see Ambrose there, talking to them.

He went back into the other room just as the porter came in.

III

"Now then," said the superintendent to the porter, "I want to see if you can throw any light on things. Sit down, man – have a cigarette?"

Plestow offered his case advisedly. He had a great notion of putting people at their ease when he questioned them. He told his particular friends that it sometimes made them careless – and that, often, there were things to be got out of a man when he was careless – things he would have kept to himself under a more rigidly conducted examination.

"You know all these gentlemen who attend this committee, I suppose?" he began.

"Very well, sir. Ever since they started meeting here about a couple of years ago. That is to say," he added, "I know their names and I know them all by sight."

"Quite so. And I imagine that, like us, you're trained to take notice of people who come in at the college gateway, eh?"

"Well, you get in the way of it, you see. It's part of my business. Of course, sir, from time to time people come in whom I don't know – visitors, and so on. But I should recognise anyone who had anything to do with the college, and – "

"And strangers?" broke in the superintendent suddenly.

"Strangers? I should know they were strangers – if that's what you mean."

"Yes. That's what I mean. Well, now. You noticed all these gentlemen when they came in this morning?"

"Just before eleven? Yes, sir. Nine of them, there were. I spoke to three or four of them."

"And you saw them go out – about one o'clock?"

"In a way I did. I was inside my lodge just then. But I couldn't swear to it that I took particular notice of them."

"I see. So that you didn't know that Mr. Hatton had remained here?"

"No, sir; I didn't."

"Very well. Now then. Between the time they arrived – eleven o'clock – and when they went out to lunch, did any strangers come in?"

"Yes. A party of four Americans."

"How do you know they were Americans?"

The porter smiled.

"We get too many of 'em here to be mistaken," he replied. "First, there was their accent and, secondly, they only stayed about six or seven minutes. On the hustle, as they always are."

"I see. Anyone else?"

"Not that I know of."

"Well, now. This is more important. These gentlemen – of the committee here – went out just before one and came back about half-past two, and during that time Mr. Hatton was murdered. You see that?"

"Certainly, sir."

The superintendent leaned forward in his chair and took his cigarette from his lips.

"Therefore, the question is, did any stranger enter and leave the college during that time?"

"Well, sir," replied the porter, "I'm afraid I can't say for certain. You see it isn't term time and, consequently, my duties are fairly slack just now. Let me see. I had a bit of dinner about one o'clock – in my lodge, and smoked a pipe afterwards. At half-past one I went out to post a parcel and was gone about five minutes. After that – well, yes, I am certain no stranger came in or went out."

"Umph! That means that from one o'clock to one thirty-five, or thereabouts, someone might have come in? But isn't there a window in your lodge?"

"Yes, sir. But, as I say, this is a slack time, and I wasn't taking any particular notice."

"That's unfortunate," replied Plestow. "Let me think a minute."

He leaned back in his chair and closed his eyes, trying to recall what the doctor had said. Yes, the doctor had seen the body at two-forty (he opened his eyes for a moment and looked at his notebook to confirm this). At two-forty. And the doctor had said that Hatton had probably been dead less than an hour before. If this were true the murderer, whoever he was, might have entered the college during the time the porter's watch was relaxed, but could he have gone out without being seen?

Again he put the question, and again the porter declared emphatically that from about one thirty-five onwards no stranger had entered or left. He pursued his inquiries. Had anyone come into the college or gone out of it between one thirty-five and two-thirty? Yes; a tradesman had come in – bringing a basket of groceries for the kitchen. The Rev. Mr. Chepstow, an old don and a member of the college, had taken in two ladies to show them round – and had left just before half-past two after staying about a quarter of an hour. Two of the college servants had gone out, and returned. And the two workmen had come in – just after two o'clock, having been out for their dinner. That was all.

Ah! Those two workmen. The superintendent scribbled a note in his pocket book. He must interview them as soon as possible. They had been at the foot of the staircase since just after two, and no one could have gone to or returned from Mr. Henlow's rooms without passing them.

"One more question," he said, looking up from his notebook. "There are, of course, the people who were in the college all the time. Who are they?"

"There are the college servants – a reduced staff. Some of them are away on holiday. And Mr. Dawson, the bursar. He's been in residence all the vacation. And Mr. Hewitt, one of the dons. He's probably been in his rooms all day. He's at work on a book, and very seldom goes out."

The superintendent shrugged his shoulders.

"I shall have to see them all," he said, "as a matter of form. You'd better let them know. Meanwhile, tell me – who looks after these rooms while Mr. Henlow is away?"

"Williams, sir, Mr. Henlow's scout."

"I see."

The superintendent got up, walked across the room and opened the door into the bedroom.

"Mr. Henlow sleeps here, I suppose?"

"When he's in residence, sir. Yes."

Once more Plestow went into the bedroom and looked round. The other followed him. More to himself than to the porter the superintendent said:

"No. I can't see that anyone could have hidden in here."

"Except in that wardrobe, sir."

"I've looked in there," said Plestow, opening the door of it again, "there are only some clothes inside – see? Well, I'll go and have a word with those workmen now."

Outside, on the little landing, he suddenly stopped. For the first time he noticed the door of the room opposite. He turned the handle. The door was locked.

"What's in there?" he asked the porter.

"It's a room that isn't used much – belongs to Mr. Henlow. He keeps books and some boxes in it."

"Where's the key?"

"I expect Williams has one."

"All right. You go and tell Williams to come along here, and bring the key of that room with him. I want to look inside."

He went down the stairs, with the porter. At the foot of them were Ambrose and the two workmen. The detective-sergeant at once said:

"I've been getting all particulars here, sir."

"Good. We'll go into that presently. But I just want to ask a question or two myself." He turned to the elder of the two men.

"What time did you begin work here this morning?"

"Seven o'clock, sir."

"What time did you go out to dinner?"

"Just before one."

"You were here all that time?"

"Me and my mate – yes, sir; both of us."

"So no one could have gone up that staircase without you seeing them?"

"Not likely."

"Who went up?"

"Only the gentlemen who came to the meeting – nine of 'em. I counted 'em."

"And the other bloke – before that," put in the younger workman.

The superintendent turned on him sharply.

"What do you mean by 'the other bloke'?" he asked. "Who was he?"

"Oh," replied the older man, "he means the chap that came along to get the rooms ready up above, one o' the college staff, he were. That's him, sir – comin' over yonder."

Plestow looked in the direction whither the other was pointing. A man was approaching from the farther end of the quad, a man of about forty, clean shaven and wearing a dark suit of clothes. The superintendent went on:

"No one else?"

"No, sir."

"What time did you two get back from your dinner?"

"Just about two o'clock."

"Who came in after that?"

"The same gentlemen as come in the morning, sir – just before the half-hour, that was."

"Did anyone come out before they arrived?"

"No, sir. I can swear to that."

The superintendent turned to the newcomer, who, by this time, was standing near by.

"You are Williams?"

"Yes, sir. The porter told me you wished to see me."

He spoke in a quiet, deferential tone of voice. The superintendent said to Ambrose:

"You say you've got all the details here – where the knife was found, and so on?"

"Yes, sir. Everything, I think."

"All right. Then you two" – and he turned to the workmen – "can get on with your job. But you can't leave the college till I give you permission. Now, Ambrose, we'll go up with Williams, please."

"The first thing I want you to do," he went on to Williams, when they arrived on the landing, "is to open that door. You've brought the key?"

"I have, sir."

He put the key in the lock and threw open the door. All three men went in.

It was a small, uncarpeted, stuffy room, redolent of the peculiar odour of books and slight dampness. A couple of cases along the walls were filled with books, more were on the floor, in piles, and there were a couple of boxes and an old suitcase.

"Mr. Henlow only has it as a lumber room," explained Williams; "he never uses it except to store books and things which he doesn't want over the way."

The superintendent nodded, looked carefully round the room, came out and, with the other two, re-entered the scene of the murder. Here he began questioning Williams.

"You act as servant to Mr. Henlow, I understand?"

"Yes, sir."

"Where is Mr. Henlow at the present moment?"

"Away in Switzerland, sir; on his holiday."

"And he lets these gentlemen – this committee – meet here?"

"Yes, sir. The first Tuesday in the month."

"Who has charge of these rooms while he is away?"

"I have, sir."

"Are they kept locked?"

"Certainly."

"Who has the key?"

"I have. As a matter of fact, it's the only key there is just now. There were two, but one got lost. Mr. Henlow gave it to me the day he went away."

"Ah!" said the superintendent; "that means that there is another key about somewhere – and that someone may have it – and could get in."

"I don't think so," replied Williams; "the other key was mine, and I know where it was lost."

"If you know where it was lost," rejoined Plestow sharply, "why haven't you found it?"

"Because I can't, sir. I was on the river with some friends in a punt, and this key and some other things fell out of my pocket when I took off my jacket – fell into the river."

"Oh! And you are certain there is no other key?"

"Not that I know of."

"Well, let that pass. So Mr. Henlow gave you his key when he went away. And how often since then have these rooms been opened – before today?"

"I couldn't exactly tell you, sir. Three or four times – to let in fresh air, and so on."

"Very well. Let us get down to today. Did Mr. Henlow tell you before he went away that you were to get things ready for the committee?"

"No, sir. But he wrote to me – from Geneva. Here's his letter. I happened to keep it and I brought it along just now, in case you might like to see it."

The superintendent read:

"Hotel de Mont Blanc,
Geneve.

August 22nd, 1931.

"DEAR WILLIAMS, – Will you please have my room ready for the Consultative Committee next Tuesday. I am writing to Mr. Pennington to tell him I shall not be back, but that the room will be at his disposal as usual.

"Also, see that those who desire it are provided with tea.

"Yours truly,

"SIDNEY HENLOW."

"Tell me," went on the superintendent, "exactly what took place this morning when you got the room ready – the exact time, too, if you can remember it."

"I unlocked the door just after half-past nine and lighted the fire – which I had laid ready last evening. It was a cold morning. I set the chairs round the table and got things generally ready."

"Did you go into the bedroom – there?"

"Yes, sir."

"What for?"

"Mr. Henlow had left me one of his overcoats to get cleaned and it had come back early this morning. I took it in his room and hung it up inside the wardrobe."

"That settles that," muttered Plestow to himself. For this made it certain that the only place in either room where a man could have hidden himself was clear.

"Go on," he said; "did you come into this room again?"

"I looked in about half-past eleven – to ask how many of the gentlemen would be staying to tea."

"And after that?"

For the first time Williams, who had been answering the superintendent's questions in a perfectly straightforward manner, hesitated a little, and his face paled.

"Well, sir," he said; "I don't want to keep anything back from you – "

"You'd better not!"

"It's this way, sir. I came in to make up the fire when the committee went out to lunch."

"Eh? What's that?" And he leaned forward. "What time did you come in?"

"Just after one o'clock, sir."

"The deuce you did! Who was here?"

"Only Mr. Hatton."

"Now be careful, Williams! This is most important. It means that you saw Mr. Hatton after Mr. Stanhope had left, and up till now, he seems to have been the last person who saw Mr. Hatton alive. Tell me exactly what happened. What was Mr. Hatton doing?"

"He was standing in front of that bookcase, with his back to me. When I came in, he turned round."

"Yes? Did he say anything?"

"I mentioned that I had come in to make up the fire. All he said was, 'All right, Williams; it's a bit cold today,' or something like that. That was all, sir."

"How long were you in the room?"

"Only a couple of minutes."

"And you left him standing by the bookcase?"

"No, sir. He moved into the window bay, over there. He didn't take any more notice of me – he was looking at a paper he had in his hand."

"A newspaper?"

"No; just a bit of paper, sir – like a half-sheet of writing paper. I couldn't say more for certain. You see, I only glanced at him."

"What did you do then?"

"I went straight back to the kitchen, and," he went on, "I can tell you the exact time when I got to the kitchen – six minutes past one."

"How do you know that?"

"Because Mr. Dawson, the bursar, was coming out of the kitchen and he asked me the right time – his watch had stopped. I'd set mine by the wireless at ten o'clock, and I looked at it and told him."

"So that, to be quite plain, you have an alibi from six minutes past one onwards?"

"Yes, sir."

Plestow frowned.

"I ought to warn you, Williams, that you are in a delicate position, I – "

"You don't suspect me, I hope, sir?"

"I never said so. On the contrary, I was about to give you a bit of advice. You will do well not to mention what you have just told me to anyone – until the inquest, when, of course, you will have to give your evidence. And I'll be perfectly fair with you. You mustn't be surprised if you find yourself under supervision for a time. There! You needn't worry," he added kindly; "we have no wish to be down on the innocent. But in my profession I take no chances. You may go now!

"He can't leave the college," he went on to Ambrose when the man had gone, "and we'll have to keep an eye on him after I allow the gate to be opened. Now then, what do you think of it, Ambrose?"

The detective-sergeant had been seated all this time, quietly smoking a pipe; listening attentively, but saying nothing. He was a man of about thirty, with dark hair and rather bald on the top of his head, clean shaven with rounded face and solemn-looking, owlish eyes, small mouth which in repose was partly open. It was a face with a peculiar wooden, vacuous expression upon it. Probably a valuable asset in his profession. For the man looked a bit of a fool. In reality, however, he was anything but that.

He was one of the types of our modern police. The son of a country clergyman, he had been educated at a public school, and afterwards, on his father's death, had found himself more or less stranded, with the discovery that even a public school education does not necessarily lead to a lucrative profession. He had knocked about the world a bit, tried his youthful hand in various pursuits, all of which had proved either temporary or uncongenial and, finally, while still in the early twenties, had joined the police force – an occupation which he did find congenial, in spite of the ordinary routine through which he had passed as a constable. Opportunities had arisen of proving his abilities in those more delicate processes of police work which call for that peculiar acumen described in modern youthful slang as "brain waves," and the Chief Constable of the county, who had a distinct flair for knowing the idiosyncrasies of the men under him, had promoted him to the post he now occupied.

He was intellectual. He was also modest. In periods of privacy he still kept in touch with those whom snobbery would have designated his "own class." With his superior officers and fellow members of the "force" he took care always to be a "policemen."

"What do you think of it, Ambrose?"

Superintendent Plestow looked questioningly at his subordinate. He, himself, was one of the modern educated, smart and up-to-date policemen. But he had, lurking in the back of his mind, the feeling that, with all his astuteness, Ambrose had a peculiar intuition which was worth attention – even if, at times, it seemed to be a trifle beside the main mark.

Ambrose removed his pipe from his mouth and said slowly:

"Well, sir, I don't think we need bother much about this chap Williams. But what he says settles the point as regards the little man with the beard who seemed to have been the last person who saw Hatton alive. He's cleared, at all events."

The superintendent's colour rose, just a trifle. The inference was that he ought to have been quite as sharp with Stanhope as he had been with Williams. He looked at the wooden, unexpressionless face of the other man. But there was no sign that he had meant such a thing.

"Yes, I know. But as a general view of the case – inside or outside? Got any opinion on that?"

"Well, all the inside people will have to be seen, of course. Even if it was an insider the question is still narrowed down to the time limit – five minutes past one till half-past two – or, rather till a few minutes after two. That was the time when the workmen returned. And no one came out afterwards. If there's anyone within the college precincts who hasn't an alibi for that period he ought to be carefully marked, of course. You've interviewed the porter, sir. What does he say about people coming in during that time?"

"He's not certain – at any rate, for the first half-hour or so."

"H'm! Anyhow, I wouldn't place too much reliance on him. It isn't term time, and these fellows are often a bit slack. Of course, someone might have come in earlier in the morning."

"I thought of that. But it's ruled out now. No one could have been hidden in these rooms before the committee met. The only place is the wardrobe in the bedroom, and Williams opened that when he came to light the fire. And the workmen down below saw no one else come in."

Ambrose thought for a few minutes. And then said:

"It's too early to form an opinion, sir, but there are one or two queer things to begin with. The first question to my mind is why didn't Hatton go out to lunch with the rest of them? He said he was going to write letters, but there's no trace of his having done so. Then, again, he didn't start eating his luncheon – that isn't touched. What was his reason for remaining here? On the face of it it looks, as if he had made an appointment with someone – in this room. The second queer thing is the disappearance of that drawing which the secretary says he left pinned on the bookcase. That's got to be accounted for. And the third queer thing is this newspaper."

Previously, while the superintendent had been questioning Williams, he had picked up and scanned a newspaper which was lying on the floor.

"That's the paper that Mr. Stanhope said Hatton was apparently reading when they found him in the chair."

"Yes, I know. But have you examined it? It's last night's *Evening Gazette*. And, what's more to the point, it's a very late edition. Look at this line or two of stop press news. It gives the result of a division in the House of Commons. Here it is. 'Second Reading of Local Rating Measure. Government majority, 91.' Now that division didn't take place till after seven."

"Well?"

"The inference is that the paper was bought late last night in London. They couldn't have got it here in time."

"It might have been posted."

"Yes; it might. And that means we've got to ask every blessed member of this committee whether he received this paper by this morning's post, and brought it along with him here. We've got their names and addresses, and I'll 'phone or write them before the day's out. But, if not – well, it's obvious that someone brought this paper from London – either last night, by a late train, or this morning. Now, the only train he could have taken last night arrives here at eleven thirty-five. The college gate would be locked by then, and they'd have to rouse up somebody to let them in. So we can easily prove that point. If no one came in after that hour – well, it looks as if someone brought the paper into this room today."

"Well, Hatton might have done that – he might have had it by post this morning and have been actually reading it when he was stabbed."

"That's possible, of course. We must ask his sister. I wish we could have been here before Stanhope removed it from the body. It might have helped. But I don't think Hatton was reading it, sir."

"Why?"

"Because if the murderer took him unawares he would probably have stabbed him through the paper. And there's no hole in it. If not, either Hatton would have been grasping it – and that's not likely, because Stanhope would probably have torn it when snatching it away – a dead man's grasp is often strong – or Hatton would have thrown it on one side. Perhaps I'm not very clear, sir, but what I mean is the paper wouldn't have been spread open, over him, as Stanhope says it was."

"But – how came it to be spread over him? Ah! I see what you mean now, Ambrose. That was clever!"

"Of course you see, sir. If anyone had come in by chance – Williams, for instance – it would have looked as if Hatton had fallen asleep by the fire, reading his paper. And they wouldn't have suspected anything or disturbed him. It's exactly what Stanhope and the other johnny thought when they came back from their luncheon. This is a cool fellow, whoever he is – calmly arranges things after he'd done the murder. Which, by the way, hardly seems to have been premeditated."

"You mean that if he used that paper-knife he hadn't brought any weapon?"

"Exactly. Snatched it off the table. Well, go on, sir. After arranging things here he hides the knife in that hole below. That must have been before two o'clock – when the workmen returned."

"And that's when he made his escape from the college?"

"Of course. If he left the college. But you say that the porter declares that from one thirty-five onwards no stranger left?"

The superintendent consulted his notebook.

"A tradesman came in and went out. Mr. Chepstow brought in two ladies, and took them out. Two of the college servants went out and returned. That's all. It begins to look as if the whole thing took place between one and one thirty-five – if it was an outsider! And yet," he went on thoughtfully, "there's a difficulty there. Look here, Ambrose, you and I and the doctor arrived here before a quarter to three, didn't we?"

"At two forty-one to be exact, sir."

"Quite so. Well, the doctor was emphatic in saying Hatton had only been dead a very short time – certainly not an hour, were his words. If that is so he couldn't have been killed before one thirty-five, could he?"

"Or after two o'clock."

"Why? Oh, yes; I see. Because the two workmen came back then, and no one left these rooms afterwards. Queer, isn't it? Is there any way a fellow could have got out of these rooms without being seen?"

Ambrose got up and walked round the room, going to each window. He went into the bedroom, and then out on the landing.

"No," he said, as he came back, "the windows looking into the quad are too high for a man to drop out – and if he did, those two workmen must have heard and seen him. There's only one way he could have got out, sir – and that isn't probable."

"What's that?"

"He could have climbed through the oriel window here, hung with his hands on the sill and dropped to the pavement below – it's not more than ten feet. But, in a crowded street, it isn't likely!"

"Um! I must have a talk with the doctor. He may be mistaken. It isn't always safe to take even expert evidence as to the exact time a man has been dead. Now, you and I will have to interview all these people within the college. It will save time if we divide them. Oh – and I've searched Hatton's pockets, there are the contents on the table. I thought I'd leave them to you. Want to look at them now?"

"No, sir. I'd rather take them and examine them at my leisure. I've brought my bag, and I'll put them in that . . . and these papers on the table?"

"I suppose they were left here by the secretary, Mr. Pennington; rough notes, seemingly."

"Anyhow, I'll take them too."

He went on putting the things in his bag. The superintendent had a final look round. Then both men went out.

Plestow locked the door of the room, and the door of the room opposite – putting both keys into his pocket. Subsequently he told Williams he had done this, and that no one was to be allowed to enter the rooms under any consideration till he had given permission.

Then he and the detective-sergeant commenced the tedious routine work of interviewing every person within the college precincts. At the end, they drew a blank. Each of the staff of servants, the bursar, and Mr. Hewitt were able to prove that they could not have been in Mr. Henlow's room between one and two o'clock. Williams was the only exception and he had already told his story.

"There!" said George Wilkins to his fellow clerk, as he looked out of the window opposite. "They've unlocked the gate over the way at last, and the superintendent has just come out. My word, Budgen, something's been going on over there! Police – ambulance – body carried out – all those johnnies leaving early! And – hallo – that's one of the *Exbridge Observer's* reporters just come up and is speaking to the bobby in the gateway! As soon as I can get out I must find out what's up."

IV

AMBROSE was seated at a table in his office at the Exbridge Police Station, carefully examining an array of articles spread out before him – the contents of the dead man's pockets. He had passed over a watch, some loose cash, and a small case containing one-pound and ten-shilling notes, a pocket knife, a bunch of keys, and so forth, and was looking through four or five letters in envelopes directed to Hatton, in the hope that he might find a clue to an appointment in Henlow's rooms on the day in question. But in this he was disappointed. There was nothing in either of the letters which could throw any light on the case.

He next turned to a small pocket diary, finding that all it contained was notes of engagements. Here, again, he met with no result. The only entry on this particular Tuesday was "Consultative Committee."

There were also the odd papers which had been left on the table in Henlow's rooms. These had evidently been used by members of the committee for making rough notes at their meetings. But there was one half-sheet of notepaper, soiled and bearing traces of having been folded in four and carried in a pocket. With the use of a magnifying glass Ambrose found two or three little bits of the "fluff" which collects in a pocket adhering to it. Also he could easily see that whereas, on the other papers, the ink was still fresh, that on this half-sheet had evidently been used some time before.

There was written on this half-sheet the following cryptic inscription:

$$\text{"3}^{rd}\text{ up} - R. - T.\text{ 3" down. } C.\text{"}$$

The detective-sergeant scrutinised it carefully, remembering as he did so that Williams, the scout, had said that when he had last seen Hatton the latter was standing in the bay of the oriel window, with what looked like half a sheet of notepaper in his hand. But he could make nothing of it, except that the two little marks above the "3" probably meant inches. Just at present, also, he had no time to attempt to solve what appeared to be a cryptogram; for he had arranged to run out to Carnford Manor that evening to interview Miss Hatton, having first telephoned to ask if she was able to receive him so soon after the shock of hearing of her brother's death.

He glanced at a post card which was among the papers before him – only the card which Henlow had sent from Geneva to Pennington. The latter had left it lying on the table.

He had just locked up all the above "exhibits" in his desk when a constable came in.

"There's a young man wishes to see you, sergeant. He asked for the Super, but the Super's out."

"Oh, I can't see him now. Turn him over to Joyce. I'm busy on this Hatton case."

"It's about that he wants to see you. When I told him the Super was out, he said he must see the next in command – he had some information."

"Very well – show him in."

Ambrose glanced at the clock on the mantelpiece a little impatiently. He knew so well, from past experience, that when a crime has been committed there are often a number of persons who, personally or by letter, volunteer "information" which subsequent investigation proves worthless. And when George Wilkins came in he was curt in his manner, and did not invite him to sit down.

"What is it?" he asked. "I can only give you a few minutes. Who are you, please?"

The young man's reply was prompt and inclusive.

"My name is George Wilkins. I am a clerk in the United Assurance Company, and my office is on the second floor of a building exactly opposite the gateway of St. Oswald's College."

"Oh!" There was a tone of interest now in his voice. "Go on, please."

"My desk is in the window of the office – I can see people going in and out of the college."

Ambrose looked at him sharply. He was rather taken with Wilkins' direct manner.

"I can also see anyone standing in the bow window that looks over the High Street."

"Eh? Well, have you seen anything today worth mentioning?"

"That's for you to say. But I thought I ought to come and tell you what I did see. I've only just heard the 'Duke' was murdered."

"The 'Duke'? What the dickens do you mean?"

"Sorry; that's only my nickname for him. You see, I've noticed these gentlemen going in over the way once a month, and I've given 'em all names – just a fancy of mine."

"Well, his name was Hatton. Now, get on with it, Mr. Wilkins – just as briefly as possible what's in your mind, and I'll ask you any questions presently – if there's anything in it."

"This morning I noticed the gentlemen going into St. Oswald's College, a little before eleven. As usual: nine of 'em. I counted them. Just about one o'clock they came out. But I didn't see the Du – Mr. Hatton, among them. But I happened to glance across the way a little later on, and there I saw him – standing at that bow window."

Ambrose thought rapidly. This was exactly in agreement with what Williams had said. There was nothing fresh.

"What time was that?" he asked.

"Thirteen minutes past one," came the prompt reply.

The detective-sergeant leaned forward in his chair with sudden interest. Williams was back in the college kitchen at six minutes past one – and had an alibi for it.

"Not thirteen minutes past," he said; "you mean earlier than that – say, three minutes?"

"No, I don't. I mean just what I said. I can swear to it."

"Why?"

"Because I was wanting my lunch – I go out for it at one-fifteen, and I looked at the office clock, which is correct. It was exactly thirteen minutes past."

"Oh! Anything else?"

"Yes. I saw him turn round all of a sudden, and then I caught just a glimpse of a chap who had gone into the college a minute or so before – only for a moment, though. Both of 'em went out of sight – out of the bow window, I mean, and – "

"Here," interrupted Ambrose, all attention now. "What's this you say about someone going into the college? Who was he?"

"Don't know. Never saw him before."

"Can you describe him?"

"Yes; what I saw of him. Elderly man with a red face and a white moustache. Wearing a brown plus-four suit and a soft hat. Looked some sort of a big wig, but not a college professor or anything like that. Carried an umbrella."

"You're observant!" said Ambrose.

Wilkins grinned at the compliment.

"I'm curious – that's what I am. And I notice things. I was only saying this morning to Budgen – a chap in my office – I ought to have been a detective. I – "

"Well," broke in Ambrose, "you're doing a bit of detective work now, and it may be useful too. Tell me more about this fellow in brown. Did you notice from what direction he came?"

"Yes. From the left."

"And went into the college?"

"Yes."

"Did he hesitate, or anything of that kind?"

"No, I don't think so."

"Did you get the impression that Hatton was expecting him – that he was watching from the window for him to come along?"

"No, I didn't. And I don't think Hatton saw him coming, either."

"Why?"

"Because of the sudden way he turned round when he was standing in the window bay – sort of start, it was."

"And then you saw this man in brown?"

"Only for half a second or so. I just caught sight of his face through the window – that was all."

"Could you identify him?"

"Yes. I think so."

"Good! Now, this is important. Did you see him go out of the college – afterwards?"

Wilkins shook his head.

"No," he replied; "I went out to get my lunch, you see, at a quarter-past one."

"When did you get back?"

"In an hour's time."

"You didn't see him – no, I suppose you wouldn't then. If only you had noticed him coming out – but there, it can't be helped. Now, look here. I want you to make a brief statement of what you've told me to a shorthand typist here, and sign it. I'll take you to his room in a moment. I shall have to see you again, but, in the meanwhile, have you told anyone else this?"

"No. I came straight to you."

"Well, keep your mouth shut then – for the present, will you, please? I'm very grateful to you for your information, and it may be important. Anyway, I'm going to act upon it immediately. Now, come along and make that statement, and sign it."

Within a very short time the description of the man who was seen by Wilkins to enter St. Oswald's College was telephoned to all stations, while every policeman in Exbridge was warned and the officials at the railway station and at the motor-coach depot were notified. So quickly was the net spread for an oldish, red-faced man with a white moustache, wearing a brown plus-four suit.

And then Ambrose started for a ten-mile run into the country – to interview the sister of the murdered man. He glanced at the little clock on the dash board of the car – half-past six.

Carnford Manor was a good-sized house in the village of that name. As Ambrose drove his car up the carriage drive from the main road he took in his surroundings. It was evident that Mr. Hatton was a man of means, the grounds were well kept and there was an air of comfortable circumstances about the whole place. He was shown into a room which was evidently the study of the murdered man, luxuriously furnished. Refinement was coupled with ease; he recognised, for he had an artistic sense, that the pictures were good. He glanced, as he waited for Miss Hatton, at the array of books in the shelves which occupied two sides of the room – standard works, poetry, belles lettres, architecture, and – here he smiled – a whole row of detective novels, seemingly quite out of place with the other literature. Then he turned. Miss Hatton had come in.

A middle-aged lady, somewhat stiff in appearance – at first sight. Intellectual face, and a very quiet, dignified manner. The word "Victorian" suggested itself to his mind.

There was just the vestige of surprise in her expression as he came forward. From a sense of duty she had consented, over the 'phone, to receive him that evening, and had expected to find an official police officer. Instead she found herself confronted with a gentlemanly looking young man, well dressed in a dark-grey suit, who came forward to meet her, easily and naturally.

"I am so sorry," he began, "to inflict myself upon you just now. I can understand what a terrible shock you have sustained and I hope you will accept my sympathy."

"Thank you," she replied. "Yes, it is very terrible. I can hardly realise it yet. Mr. Kershaw was very kind in coming here to break the news to me this afternoon. Won't you sit down, Mr. – ?"

"I am Detective-Sergeant Ambrose. It is very good of you to see me – so soon."

"I felt I ought to do so. Though I hardly know how I can help you."

"You may be able to help me very much, Miss Hatton, if you will let me ask you some questions. I would like to make it plain to you that I'm not going to be inquisitive simply out of curiosity, but from a professional point of view. We naturally want to solve this horrible crime and see justice done. And in a case like this it often helps us if we are able to probe into personal matters – not necessarily for publication. So I am going to ask you to give me your confidence."

"I will try to tell you anything you may ask me."

"Thank you. Now you saw your brother before he went to Exbridge this morning?"

"Of course – we had breakfast together."

"Was there anything unusual in his manner before he started?"

"Why, no."

"May I ask what he talked about?"

"Mostly about the meeting to which he was going. He always looked forward to these meetings of the Consultative Committee. He was exceedingly keen on ecclesiastical architecture, and was in his element with the little group of friends he met at Exbridge every month."

"Was there any particular matter concerning the meeting which he mentioned?"

"Yes – there was. He was joking about an absurd stained-glass window that was designed for some church in the diocese. I think he told me which church it was, but I don't remember it now. I do remember, however, that he said he was sure the committee would never sanction the scheme, and that Mr. Stanhope – one of the members – would have a fit when he saw the design of the window."

"I see. Now – tell me this, if you will. It seems to be the custom of the members of the Consultative Committee to lunch at restaurants. But, unfortunately, your brother didn't do so today."

"I know. He took his luncheon with him. He asked me to tell the cook to cut some sandwiches for him before he went."

"Exactly. Now, had he ever taken his luncheon with him before?"

"N-no – not that I remember."

"Did he give any reason for taking it?"

"No."

"Didn't you ask him?"

"No. He was just going out of the breakfast room when he mentioned it. And I never saw him again."

"Didn't it strike you as rather peculiar – this taking his luncheon with him?"

"I don't think so. And I cannot quite understand why you should ask?"

"Because of this," replied Ambrose gravely. "On the face of it it looks as if your brother may have made an appointment – an appointment with someone who was to meet him in Mr. Henlow's rooms at St. Oswald's during the luncheon hour. And my next question is very important. Did he, in any way, give you the slightest cause to imagine that he was going to meet someone?"

"Not for a moment – no – I'm sure he didn't."

"And yet, Miss Hatton, we already have a very good reason to believe that someone did visit him, a little after one o'clock, when he was alone in Mr. Henlow's rooms."

"Indeed? Who was it?"

"That we don't know yet. I hope we shall. But I have his description. This is it."

And he told her.

She thought for a few moments, carefully.

"No – " she said, slowly, "I certainly do not recognise your description as that of any of my brother's friends. But – of course – he knew a number of people with whom I am unacquainted. Do you think, then," she went on, her voice breaking a little, "that this was the man – who – who killed him?"

"That we cannot say at present. But, so far as we know he was the only person who could have had the opportunity of doing so."

"But why – oh, why did anyone want to do such a wicked thing?"

"Ah, Miss Hatton, if we only knew that, it would mean the solution of everything."

"He hadn't an enemy in the world, that I know of."

"Unfortunately most of us have enemies, of some sort, that we don't know of."

"But I can't imagine that anyone – " She broke off. "Have you any idea?"

He shook his head.

"I want to find out, Miss Hatton. And it is just here that you can possibly help me most. I want you to tell me about your brother, so that I can get some idea of his personality. For example, his life here – his habits? Can you give me a brief outline? You have lived with him for some time, I suppose?"

"For ten years. I came to him here when his wife died. They had no children. With the exception of occasional short holidays we have been together ever since. He was comfortably off and able to satisfy his tastes – which were simple. He was devoted to art – architecture, chiefly; and read and wrote here a great deal. Most of his friends were in the art world, and he belonged to several societies – antiquarian, and so forth. But he spent most of his time, quietly, here."

"Had he any other hobbies?"

"He took a great interest in the garden."

Ambrose glanced at the bookcase.

"One often judges a man by his library," he said. "I was looking at those books just now – and, if I may say so, Mr.

Hatton seems to have had an interest in other objects than art. Apparently he was fond of detective stories."

She smiled faintly.

"Yes – he was. He often read them, the last thing at night. He used to say they rested his brain, but I never could see how they could do that. On the contrary, they excited his imagination."

"Perhaps that was why they rested his brain – by turning it in another direction."

"I don't know. I always said they worried him."

"Why?"

"Because, you see, he never read a story straight through to the end. He used to try to solve what he called the problem. I've known him spend a week – I mean the time after dinner, working out solutions – with a pencil and a note pad. And then he'd turn to the end of the book to see if he was right. Only last week, for three evenings, I could hardly get a word out of him."

"And did he solve the problem he was working at?" asked Ambrose, his mind going off at a tangent now that his own particular subject was prominent.

"Oh, yes. I remember him saying, suddenly, 'I've got it at last!' And, even then, he went on brooding over it."

"After he'd referred to the book?"

She thought for a few moments.

"He – no, he didn't refer to the story – as he usually did. But, surely – this is hardly of interest to you –"

"I am sorry. You aroused my professional curiosity."

He asked her a few more questions – ending with a query as to who were Hatton's closest friends. She told him, so far as she knew. Pennington and Stanhope figured among them. They were all connected with the art world."

"Oh," she added, "and he had a great friend in Exbridge – Dr. Blake, the Lady Purbeck Professor of Divinity. They frequently met."

"Thank you," he said, getting up from his chair. "It is very good of you to have let me come this evening. I won't worry you any further now. Only" – he hesitated a little – "it sometimes happens in distressing cases of this kind that one may gather a hint from any papers – notes, and so on – "

"I think I understand. Of course I shall have to go through everything. I am his sole surviving relative, and he told me some time ago that he had made me one of his executors. If I should find anything that seems to bear on the tragedy I shall remember what you say. And perhaps I had better keep this room locked for the present."

"I was going to suggest that. Goodnight. Please let me say that, quite apart from my official capacity, you have my very real sympathy. And if I can help you in any way, please let me know."

"I am not revengeful, I trust," she replied, "yet I cannot but wish that you will succeed – in your official capacity."

"You may be sure we shall do our best, Miss Hatton."

V

IT was half-past eight that evening when Ambrose returned to the police station and sought the superintendent. Before he could give any report of his interview with Miss Hatton, however, Plestow began:

"Look here, Ambrose," he said, "there's a fresh development – at least, what may be so. I've just had a 'phone message from Jennings, the constable at Little Marpleton. He came back to his house after a country round half an hour ago and found the description you circulated of that chap in a brown knickerbocker suit – his wife had taken it down. And he says it looks very much like the squire there – old Matthew Finmere. Says he saw Mr. Finmere at Little Marpleton station this morning, dressed like that."

"Who is Mr. Finmere, sir? I've never heard of him."

"Haven't you? Oh, I know him – so does everyone round Little Marpleton way. He's a magistrate, among other things – sits on the bench at Derringford, and is a holy terror if he gets a poacher before him – would sentence him to be hanged, if he could. Quite a county magnate: owns a big place at Little Marpleton and half the village, too. Rules locally with a rod of iron. Old-fashioned country squire with a big idea of his own importance and the very devil of a temper. Got into trouble a couple of years ago for striking a farm labourer with his hunting crop – no – he wasn't prosecuted, but he had to pay for hushing it up. Well, that's the fellow who Jennings thinks is your man, and if he's right, Ambrose, we're going to have trouble."

"Have you given Jennings any instructions about it, sir?"

"No, I haven't. He isn't the man to tackle old Finmere. If the squire's mixed up in this affair we'll have to go to work carefully. He's a clever old blighter – apart from his temper. And if he did stick Hatton for some reason or other it won't be too easy to prove it. Now, are you very tired?"

"Oh, never mind that, sir."

"All right. Well, if you let her rip you could run your car over to Little Marpleton in half an hour. I wish you'd go and see old Finmere at once. I don't think we ought to put it off."

"Neither do I, sir. I'll go now."

"And – look here. If you think there's any reason to be suspicious, tell Jennings to keep an eye on Mr. Finmere's movements. He's capable of that – just to let us know if the old man leaves the village. He hasn't got a car, I know – much too old-fashioned to keep one – so if he does try to make a getaway it'll be by train. Right, then – I'll be here when you get back. The Chief's coming to see me at half-past nine."

The "Chief" being Colonel Langdale, the Chief Constable of the county.

Once more Ambrose started off in his car, and "let her rip." It was still daylight, and the way to Little Marpleton was, for the most part, not a very much frequented highway. He met very little traffic, and it was only a quarter-past nine when he found himself in the private carriage drive leading to Marpleton Manor House.

The Manor House was a large, substantial building of red brick, with a flight of stone steps leading up to a massive portico. Ambrose got out of his car and rang the bell. After rather a long interval the door was opened by the butler, who, so Ambrose noticed, was wearing a morning coat and waistcoat.

"Is Mr. Finmere in?"

"Mr. Finmere is away from home, sir."

"Oh! I wanted to see him rather particularly. When will he be back?"

"I can't say for certain, sir – not for a fortnight or three weeks, I think."

"Indeed? I suppose you couldn't give me his address – so that I could write to him?"

"No, sir. He didn't leave it with me. He's gone abroad, sir."

"Gone abroad?"

"Yes, sir – only today."

"And he didn't tell you where he was going?"

"Mr. Finmere never does that, sir. But sometimes when he is away he has occasion to write to me. If he does so, I could forward any message – if you care to leave one."

"Oh – it doesn't matter."

"Who shall I say called, sir?"

"Oh, well – that doesn't matter either. Goodnight."

"Goodnight, sir."

Ambrose was turning to go. The butler was in the act of shutting the door when he hesitated, opened it again, and came out on the portico.

"Mr. Finmere may have told Mr. Rudge where he was going, sir."

Ambrose, half-way down the steps, turned once more.

"Mr. Rudge?"

"The vicar, sir. I know Mr. Finmere was at the vicarage last evening."

"Oh – thank you. Very well. Where is the vicarage?"

"Turn to your left when you get out on the road, sir – it's the second house on the right – stands a little way back – near the church."

Ambrose found the vicar in his study, smoking a pipe and reading – a thin, melancholy-looking man, middle-aged, with rather a weak, receding chin, and a slight nervousness of manner. Ambrose introduced himself.

"I am sorry to disturb you at such a late hour, sir," he began, "but I am trying to get some information with regard to a serious crime which was committed at Exbridge today."

"Crime? What crime?"

"Apparently murder, sir."

"Dear me, dear me! That's very terrible. Who was it?"

"A Mr. Hatton, sir."

"Hatton? You don't mean Mr. Francis Hatton – of Carnford?"

Ambrose nodded.

"Yes, sir. That's the man."

"Murdered, you say? Horrible, horrible! Why he was here only a few days ago – we gave him tea. How did it happen? Do tell me."

Ambrose told him, as briefly as possible. The vicar said:

"I trust you will be able to find the miscreant. But how can I help you? I hardly knew Mr. Hatton. I think I only met him once before he came here last week. And I really know very little about him."

"That isn't the point, sir. We are not at all certain, but we have reason to believe that one of your parishioners may have seen him today in the room in St. Oswald's College where the Consultative Committee of the diocese meet."

"Mr. Henlow's room?"

"Exactly. And," went on Ambrose, "that this same parishioner, if he did see him there, must have been with him very shortly before he was murdered – must have been, in fact, the last person who saw him alive."

"But, surely," said the vicar, "it would be best for you to see this parishioner of mine yourself, wouldn't it? Who is – ?"

"I've just endeavoured to do so, sir. But he's away from home. He's the squire here, Mr. Firunere. His butler does not know his address and advised me that you might have it."

"Oh, dear, oh, dear!" exclaimed the vicar, nervously tapping the table with his fingers. "Mr. Finmere? What in the world – ?" He stopped short. "You can't imagine that he had anything to do with this terrible affair, I hope?"

"I never said so, sir. But if he was with Mr. Hatton at the time I mentioned it stands to reason that I must get hold of him and interview him."

"If he was with Mr. Hatton, you say? Dear me! But how very awkward!"

"What's very awkward, sir?" asked the detective-sergeant, a little sharply. "What makes you say that?"

"Because – well – really, you know, I don't want to be mixed up in this affair, sergeant. I've nothing to do with it. And I don't know where Mr. Finmere is, either. Except that he's gone abroad – he was leaving by the night boat train for Paris, where he was to stay two or three days. And then he talked of going on to Evian-les-Bains. But he wasn't certain. And he said nothing about any particular hotel."

"I'm obliged to you for the information, Mr. Rudge," replied Ambrose. "But I must still ask you why you said it is very awkward about Mr. Finmere being with Mr. Hatton."

"Well – it is, isn't it? I mean, people might gossip – And Finmere might think I told you – er – that is to say – "

"Told me what, sir? I'm sorry, but I must ask you to be a little more explicit. This is a very serious affair, and if you know anything which may throw the very slightest light upon it – well, I need hardly tell you, sir, that you must not keep it back from me."

"But I don't know anything, really – that is to say – I only thought – "

"Yes, sir? What?"

The vicar suddenly made up his mind, with, like most weak people, the air of a man who could not help himself.

"Well, to be quite frank with you – and it is not a pleasant subject – I was thinking of Mr. Finmere's unfortunate temper. He sometimes loses it on very little provocation. And – if he saw Hatton, as you say he did – "

"No," broke in Ambrose, "I never went so far as that. I only said we have certain reasons for believing that he might have seen him. I will go further than that. We have a description of an individual who was with Mr. Hatton just before his death – and the description seems to tally with that of your squire."

"I – I have no doubt it does. You see – well – I suppose I had better tell you. I happen to know that, in all probability, Mr. Finmere meant to go to St. Oswald's College today – on his way to London."

The detective-sergeant leaned forward. He was getting at something tangible – at last.

"And how do you know that, Mr. Rudge?"

"Because he told me so – last evening. Look here – I'll try to make it plain – er – I am speaking in strict confidence."

"Stop a minute, sir – please! You must bear in mind that, in my official capacity, I can promise no confidence beyond a certain limit. In the interests of justice it is your duty to tell me what you know, but I should not be treating you fairly unless I warned you that it is quite possible that you may have to repeat your statement at the inquest."

"Dear, dear! I wouldn't have had this happen for – well, there's no disguising the fact, but my position is an awkward one. I have no wish to fall out with Mr. Finmere – he is the squire of my parish and the patron of the living, you see."

Ambrose shrugged his shoulders.

"It's not always easy to take the line of duty, sir," he said. "I dare say you've sometimes preached on that."

The vicar reddened. The shaft had gone home.

"Very well," he said. "I suppose I'd better tell you – without any conditions. It all came about, you see, from a memorial – a stained-glass window – that Mr. Finmere wished to put up in my church in memory of his wife. I am bound to admit that he was obstinate in the way he set about it. I warned him that there were certain diocesan authorities who would have to be satisfied that the memorial was a suitable one, but he would not listen. Without consulting anyone he commissioned an artist of his acquaintance to design the window – and to make it. I confess that I was disappointed when I saw the design, but – well – it was passed unanimously by our Parochial Church Council, and we applied to the Chancellor of the Diocese for a faculty to put it up."

"Now the chancellor referred the matter to the Consultative Committee and they sent one of their members – this poor fellow Hatton – here. He came last week, as I told you. He and Mr. Finmere and I went into the church, and I am sorry to say Mr. Finmere lost his temper. You see,

Hatton told him plainly that he didn't think for a moment that the committee would pass the design, and tried to persuade him to consult another artist – nominated by the committee. The squire was furious, and would not listen to Hatton's advice. He even went so far as to say that he would put the window in the church, faculty or no faculty. It ended by Hatton saying that he was going to report to the committee when it met at St. Oswald's College today – and – pointing out again – that he felt sure the scheme would be turned down."

"That was last Wednesday, and I suppose Mr. Finmere has been thinking over it since. Anyhow, he came to see me last night about the matter. He was still very angry – and it was painful to me to have to listen to his remarks about Hatton. Well, he told me that he wasn't going to be coerced either by the Consultative Committee or by the chancellor, and that as it was pretty plain that they would not sanction the design, he had altered his plans. He would still have the window – which was actually in the course of construction – but, instead of putting it in the church, he meant to have it erected in his own dining-room, and that, when he returned from abroad, he should see a builder and get the artist to come down here to consult with him. Meanwhile – and this is the point I have been driving at – he said he was going to fetch away the design from the committee before they had a chance of thwarting him by turning it down. Hatton, as I said, had told him the committee was meeting today, so he meant to take a morning train to Exbridge, get the design, take it up to London with him, and see the artist before he left for the Continent."

Ambrose was listening attentively. One of the queer things in connection with the case was being solved – the disappearance of that design which Pennington said he had left pinned to the bookcase in Henlow's room, and which he could not find on his return there.

The vicar proceeded.

"Mr. Finmere," he said, "asked me to tell him whereabouts in St. Oswald's College the committee met. Now, I knew that Henlow let them have his room for their meetings, and I knew exactly where his room was. In fact, I've often been in it myself. When I was up at Exbridge as an undergraduate I had a friend who had those rooms then, and, besides, I have occasionally visited Henlow there – we are interested in the same subject – Greek mythology – and he is good enough to consult my little store of knowledge sometimes, when he is working on one of his books."

"So what I did was this. I drew a rough plan of the two quads, and showed Finmere the way to Henlow's rooms. I remember saying to him last evening, 'You can't go wrong – through the archway on the right of the first quad – turn right – and you'll see the doorway of Henlow's staircase straight in front of you – in the corner of the inner quad!' There! I've told you all I know."

"I am greatly obliged to you, sir. And I can't see that you have any cause for worrying – "

"There is Finmere's excitable temper – he may have given way to it – "

"Even if he did – it can hardly concern you."

"No. But he may be furious with me for telling you this, and – "

"I'm afraid you must make up your mind to chance that, sir. Besides, we don't know yet if he did go to Henlow's rooms. Though we can soon find out."

"How?"

"Well – have you the address of this artist who designed the window?"

The vicar opened a drawer in the study table at which he was seated.

"Yes – here it is – S. W. Hastings, 3A Amberley Road, St. John's Wood."

"Good! He'll be able to tell us if Mr. Finmere called on him today with the design. If he did – well, that will prove it. Now, I want to ask you a question that may seem peculiar. You know Mr. Finmere very well, of course. Can you tell me what daily papers he takes in?"

"Daily papers? Why, so far as I know, he never reads any paper but *The Times*. Why do you ask?"

Ambrose evaded the question by asking another. "You don't know whether he had an evening paper posted to him from London?"

"I really can't say. If he does I've never seen one in his house."

"I see."

He reflected a little. It was obvious that each member of the committee would have to be asked whether he had brought the *Evening Gazette* with him to the meeting. He had already, in his interview with Miss Hatton, asked her whether her brother had it posted to him, her reply being a negative.

"And you say," he went on, "that Mr. Finmere told you he was probably going to Evian-les-Bains?"

"He said he might do so – after staying a few days in Paris."

"Well," said Ambrose, getting up from his chair, "I won't disturb you any further. Thank you very much for the information you have given me."

"And the inquest?" asked the vicar, as he took the detective-sergeant to the front door. "Shall I really have to attend?"

"Not at present at all events. When it first opens – on Thursday, I think – the proceedings will only be formal. We shall ask for an adjournment and I will let you know. Goodnight, sir."

Before returning to Exbridge, Ambrose called on Jennings, the local policeman. He found that worthy having his supper – in his shirt sleeves.

"We had your 'phone message," explained Ambrose.

"Yes, sergeant – anything wrong about the old squire here?"

"I can't say at present. What time did he go to Exbridge this morning?"

"By the twelve-fourteen train from here. I happened to be at the station. Had a couple of suitcases with him."

"I want you to find out something."

"What's that, sergeant?"

"D'you know the postman here?"

"Very well indeed. We often have a talk together."

"Well – manage to knock up against him – accidentally – and find out casually whether he delivers a newspaper at the Manor House every morning – by the first post."

"All right. I can easily do that."

"'Phone the result at once."

"Right, sergeant."

When Ambrose returned to the police station at Exbridge it was getting on for eleven o'clock. But he found the superintendent, at that late hour, still in his office, and Colonel Langdale with him.

The chief constable was a tall, thin man with iron-grey hair, a little bald on the top of his head, and clean-shaven. He had a pleasant, thoughtful-looking face, rather dreamy grey eyes, and spoke in a very cultured, soft tone of voice, with a slight drawl. He listened attentively while Ambrose recounted his interview with the vicar, and then remarked to the superintendent:

"You will, of course, follow this up?"

"Certainly, sir. We must get at this artist fellow to begin with. If Mr. Finmere did go and see him today he may be a help. But, of course, we must follow up Finmere – somehow."

"I suppose so," drawled the colonel, "but it is an exceedingly awkward situation. I know Finmere very well – and his temper, too. But that it led him to commit murder, well! –" and he shrugged his shoulders.

"The facts are awkward," put in the superintendent.

"They are – oh, yes, they certainly are," said the colonel. "Well, I must be getting home – oh, by the way" – and he turned to the superintendent – "before I go, I must mention quite another matter. Have you or Detective-Inspector Hilton any information yet with regard to that wretched business of these robberies at Exbridge?"

"I wish we had, sir. I've done my best – and so has Hilton, but we don't seem to get hold of the slightest clue."

"So I understand. I wish you could. It's not only a mystery – but our reputation's at stake. Five of them now!" He ticked them off on his fingers. "First the Warmingham Missal, taken from the Maxham College library – that was just over a year ago. Secondly the Apollo Statuette – from the Brendon Museum. Then that miniature – from Dr. Blake's private collection. After that, what was it that was missing – from the Brendon Museum, again? Ah, yes – that little Etruscan vase. And, lastly, only a month ago, the Corot – cut out of the frame – hanging in the Provost's dining-room at Malvern College. This is no ordinary criminal. He knows what to go for, and he knows his hunting ground."

"And they are all fairly small objects," said the superintendent.

"Precisely. That Corot was only a small picture. But who gets them? – that's the point. Who gets them?"

"You mean – ?" began Plestow.

"I mean," went on the chief constable, "that they can't be disposed of in the ordinary way. Either the fellow is a collector himself, with a warped sense of meum and tuum – or – well, there are other collectors – with the same sense of possession at all hazards at the cost of honesty. I mustn't stay any longer – but I just want to be sure – you think Ambrose, here, had better centre on this murder case?"

"Yes. I do, sir," replied the superintendent. "Unless, of course, you wish me to call in Scotland Yard?"

"I think I'll give you a chance first."

"Thank you, sir. Well, I shall keep Hilton on the robberies – he's a sharp fellow. But you know that the museum officials have consulted a private agency – and I heard that Dr. Blake hinted that he was doing the same?"

"Yes – I know. Well, see to it, superintendent, that they don't cut you out. Plenty of sharp fellows in these agencies, they tell me – and not hampered by beastly restrictions as we are. Goodnight – goodnight, Ambrose, and I wish you luck"

VI

AMBROSE woke the next morning with the consciousness that he had a busy day before him. There was a fast train to London a little before eleven, but, before going to interview the artist, he wanted to make a complete examination of Mr. Henlow's rooms. He called in at the police station first. The previous day he had instituted inquiries concerning the evening paper found spread over the murdered man's body. Results had only come in from those members of the committee who were on the telephone – all of them denied that they had taken any evening paper to the meeting. Then he made his way to St. Oswald's College, and let himself into Henlow's rooms with the key which was in his possession.

Nothing, of course, had been touched since the room had been locked up the previous afternoon. There were plenty of traces of its occupation by the members of the committee, sundry cigarette ends and tobacco ashes and shreds in the two ash trays on the table, and in the grate, a few bits of yellowish clay earth on the floor – of course, that meant that they had carried it in on their boots from below the stairs; he remembered that pile of yellowish soil heaped up alongside the hole that had been dug – stray bits were lying about still at the foot of the staircase – he even flicked one off from his own shoe as he glanced down at it. No help here – every one who had come into that room the day before had probably left this particular trace behind him

Methodically he examined every portion of the room. Two of the windows had sash frames, and were fastened with the usual hasp. One casement of the oriel window opened, on hinges, inwards, but was secured by a snap fastening – in fact, he had himself closed it the day before, for it seemed to have been open during the committee meeting. He remembered that Williams had said that when he came in to look to the fire, Hatton had been standing in front of the bookcase. So he turned his attention to it. On the floor at the foot of the bookcase three or four drawing pins were lying. Well, the design of that window had been pinned on the case, and that accounted for them.

There was a layer of dust on the shelves – in front of the rows of books – but in one place, this dust had evidently been disturbed. Closer examination made it plain that four or five volumes must have been pulled out, thus scraping the dust. He took out, very carefully, two of these books, and went to the window to examine them. On the upper portion of each some dust had accumulated, but was slightly rubbed off near the back, just as would happen if a finger was laid on the top of a book when pulling it out of the case. Three of the other volumes, those next to the first two, were similarly marked.

He looked at their titles. Two were Henlow's own works, *Modern Statecraft in the Light of Plato's "Republic,"* and *Lectures on the Ethical Ideals of Plato*. Of the others, one was a Tennyson, the next *Highways and Bye-ways of Downshire*, and the third a volume of reminiscences by a lately retired judge. Well, if Hatton had been consulting those five books for any specific purpose the combination of subjects would be difficult to determine!

He next turned his attention to a waste-paper basket that stood beside the table. Here, again, he drew a blank. There were only a few bits of paper containing evident jottings by the members of the Consultative Committee.

He went outside this room – on the staircase. There were similar fragments of earth on the bare stairs, but nothing to be gained from them. He unlocked the door of the lumber room opposite – and went in. A few similar bits of yellowish clay there. Of course, he and the superintendent and Williams had all been in that room the previous afternoon when Williams had brought the key to open it.

Lastly he went into the bedroom and carefully examined it. Again – nothing! He opened the door of the wardrobe, mechanically. There was plenty of room for a man to have hidden himself there, but, of course, that was out of the question. The superintendent had examined that wardrobe soon after he had arrived. There was the array of clothes hanging up in it. He stood in front of it, trying to think out the sequence of events. The present obvious solution was that Finmere had committed the crime in one of his ungovernable fits of temper. Everything pointed to that. But, suppose that this supposition was wrong, how could anyone else have got into those rooms and escaped afterwards without being seen? Take, first of all, the getting in. From the moment that those two workmen had begun their job at the foot of the stairs early on the previous morning until about twenty minutes past one – which was about the earliest time that Finmere would have left Hatton alone once more (still supposing that Finmere was innocent) the thing was impossible.

Still, suppose – further – that the murderer had come in before the workmen appeared on the scene, very early in the morning – or even overnight. Suppose he knew, beforehand, that Hatton intended to stay by himself during the luncheon hour – for it was pretty evident that Hatton had, for some reason or other, planned to do this – and had purposely waited there for hours in order not to be seen by the porter, or others coming in during the luncheon hour. Where would he have been during the time the committee was sitting? Obviously in that bedroom – for the room on the other side of the landing was locked, and Williams had the key. But it would not have been safe for him to have remained, openly, in the bedroom because – Ambrose remembered it now – Williams had told him and the superintendent, among other things – that he always provided water in the bedroom jug in case any of the committee wished to wash their hands – as they sometimes did. The murderer might not, it was true, have known that, but anyway, he would not be likely to have run the risk of anyone coming in from the other room and finding him there. The inference was, then, that he might have hidden himself, during the sitting of the committee, in that wardrobe. True, Williams said he had opened the wardrobe when he came into the rooms to light the fire; but the murderer might, at that time, have been in the outer room. There was plenty of space behind the curtain across the bay of the oriel window for him to have eluded Williams for the few moments the latter was there. Afterwards, as the time of the committee meeting approached, he could have made for the wardrobe. Rather a far-fetched notion, but possible. Supposing it to be possible – were there any traces?

The detective-sergeant went down on his knees and looked closely on the floor of the wardrobe. Three pairs of shoes stood there, side by side, perfectly clean. Williams, evidently, knew the art of getting a good shiny polish on the leather. There was only one slight peculiarity about them – one shoe had no lace in it. The next moment, however, Ambrose caught sight of a short, broken lace, lying in a corner on the floor of the wardrobe. There was also another small object which caught his eye as he bent down – something brilliantly red, with a black end. One of those small, flat paper matches which are sold in folders convenient for the waistcoat pocket – a match which had been struck and partly burnt. It was a red match and had something printed on it, just the latter part of a word. The rest had been burnt. The letters were "TAINE." More from habit than for any particular reason, Ambrose put both the bit of bootlace and the used match in one of the little envelopes he carried for preserving what he called "possible exhibits." Habit, because it was one of his methods to collect all seemingly trivial objects on the scene of a crime, in case one of them might be connected with it. Thus, he had already collected the drawing pins lying at the foot of the bookcase, the bits of paper in the waste-paper basket, two or three dollops of the yellowish earth, and so forth.

He rose to his feet, however, with a strong sense of disappointment. After all, it was quite impossible that the theory of anyone being hidden in that wardrobe – or in that room, could be practicable. For, even if it were so, how could the fellow have got out? That was the crux, after all. No one was in that bedroom – or in the room across the landing when the murder was discovered. That was quite certain. And no one had left the college without the porter knowing of it after one-thirty-five. And no one had come down the stairs while the two workmen were there. Therefore, if the murderer had been hidden in the bedroom beforehand, and – as it followed – Finmere had nothing to do with the crime – the deed must have been committed in an incredibly short space of time. The clerk over the way had caught a glimpse of Finmere through the oriel window at thirteen minutes past one. Ostensibly Finmere had gone to Henlow's rooms to get the design of the window. Well, it would take him a few minutes to remove it from the bookshelf and roll it up. At the very earliest he would leave at about one-twenty, possibly a few minutes later. That would give only about ten minutes for the murderer to come in from the bedroom, stab Hatton, carefully arrange the body in the chair with the newspaper spread over it, hide – as he thought – the paper-knife in the loose earth in the hole at the foot of the stairs – go through the two quads and out of the gate before one-thirty-five. No! It was preposterous.

One last look around, and Ambrose locked up the rooms once more and left the college. There was still a little time before his train started. He crossed the street, entered the offices of the United Assurance Company, saw the branch manager and explained his errand, and asked to be allowed to go into George Wilkins' room. Here he made that would-be detective show him exactly the position of affairs opposite. And he saw how easily anyone standing in the oriel window of Henlow's room could be recognised from Wilkins' vantage point. Again he questioned the young clerk sharply about the exact time – but Wilkins was still emphatic. He had seen "the blighter in the brown togs" exactly at one-thirteen – in that room opposite.

"Do you think you'll get him?" he asked, eagerly.

Ambrose smiled.

"We may."

"And then he'll be hanged, eh?"

"You are too precipitate, my friend. We're not sure yet if he's the right man – and, even if he is, there is such a thing as proving it – to say nothing of what a jury may think. I still want you to keep quiet about the matter."

"But – the inquest – ?"

"That's tomorrow. But we shan't want you then. There will be an adjournment, and any evidence you may have to give will be taken later on. I'll let you know."

Ambrose proceeded to the station, and caught the London train. He found Hastings at work in his studio at St. John's Wood, introduced himself, and explained his errand, taking care, however, not to arouse the artist's suspicion.

"We are under the impression," he said, "that Mr. Finmere may help us in solving this case. We are pretty well sure that he must have been with Mr. Hatton just before the latter was murdered, and from other information we think he may have come on to you afterwards."

Hastings was an untidy-looking man of about five-and-forty, with a shock of yellow hair and a short beard, wearing an overall. His fingers were stained – evidently he had been using dye in the process of colouring glass.

"Yes, yes," he said, "that is quite right. He called here yesterday – in the late afternoon."

"I see. Now, would you mind telling me why he called – and whether he happened to mention that he had been to St. Oswald's College before he left Exbridge?"

"Why, of course he did. That was his reason for coming here. You see he had commissioned me to design and execute a memorial window to the late Mrs. Finmere – to be put in Little Marpleton Church. I'd sent him the design – some weeks ago, and he approved of it. But there seems to have been some difficulty about a faculty. Anyhow, he brought back the design yesterday and said he'd changed his mind – he meant to put the window in his house instead of in the church. He came to talk it over with me, as, of course, there were several new points to be considered. I tried to reason with him, but he was very determined, and the end of the matter was that I was to run down to his place in a few weeks' time to consult with a builder. I can't imagine," he went on, "why there was any fuss about a faculty – I've never had anything turned down by a church before – but, from what Mr. Finmere told me, there's a beastly interfering committee of amateurs, who think they know – "

"Yes, yes," broke in Ambrose, "but now – you say he brought you this design. Did he tell you he went to St. Oswald's College to get it?"

"I was going to explain," replied Hastings, a little testily. "This committee – the design was to come before them at a meeting yesterday, he said. The Chancellor of the Diocese had sent it on to them. But Mr. Finmere having, as I say, changed his mind, went to them yesterday to fetch the design and bring it to me."

"And did he tell you – well, who he saw there?"

"Yes, he did. And he wasn't very complimentary either."

"What did he say?"

"That there was only one member of the committee there – the others had gone out to lunch."

"Did he say who that member was?"

"He didn't mention his name. What he did say was that he'd found the damned fool who had visited Little Marpleton Church a few days before, and that he'd told him what he thought of him and the rest of his confounded committee. Those were his words as nearly as I can recollect. Oh, yes – and he said he'd found my design fixed on a bookcase with drawing pins, and – he doesn't mince words, you know – and that the damn things had been pressed in so tightly he'd had to use a steel paper knife that was lying on the table to force them out."

"What made him tell you that, I wonder?"

"I suppose because he'd torn a bit out of the design. He explained that the knife had slipped. But it was of no consequence, really."

The detective-sergeant considered. The artist had, unconsciously, suggested a denouement that very possibly might have happened. The irascible old squire, with the knife in his hand, storming and swearing at Hatton. The latter making sarcastic retorts – about the design of the window. The sudden impulse, born of passion – the unpremeditated blow – the consequent sobering effect on Finmere, the quick working of his brain, the arranging of the body, the retreat down the stairs, the hiding of the weapon. All taking place within the time limit – before one-thirty-five.

That morning, before he left Exbridge, he had received the report concerning finger-print tests on the knife. But it was a hopeless report. The workman who had found the knife had destroyed any evidence there might have been – he had handled it, wiped the dirt off it, and kept it loose in his pocket till he had given it to Stanhope.

He asked a further question of the artist.

"What time did Mr. Finmere leave you yesterday?"

"About half-past five."

"Did he tell you where he was going?"

"Yes. He was taking the evening boat-train. He said he was going to Paris – and afterwards probably to Haute Savoie."

"Did he mention the route?"

"No."

Again Ambrose pondered. Late the previous night, when he had made his report to the superintendent, the latter had seen to it, on the telephone, that the Channel ports were advised, and that a message went through to the Sûreté in Paris to keep a watchful eye on Mr. Finmere, should he be identified on his journey by his passport. But if he had taken the short route to the Continent, by the early evening boat-train, he would have reached Calais before the message had been received, and it might be difficult to trace him.

He asked a few more questions of the artist, and then left. The inner man reminded him that even detectives must eat, and, hailing a taxi, he gave the driver the name of one of those little Bohemian restaurants in Soho where a decent meal may be had at a trifling cost – a restaurant which he frequented when business or pleasure brought him to London.

It was past the usual rush for luncheon when he arrived, and only about a dozen people were seated at the little tables in the long, narrow room which the restaurant boasted. One man, a little bearded man, smoking a big briar pipe over his coffee, seemed familiar to Ambrose. He looked at him – the recognition was mutual. It was Stanhope. The detective-sergeant paused, greeted the little artist, who responded by indicating with a gesture that there was a vacant place at his table, inviting him to take it. Ambrose did so.

"Curious we should meet again so soon," said Stanhope.

"Not at all," retorted Ambrose. "We live in a world of coincidences, and if they didn't happen in my line of work sometimes, I should be at a dead end."

The waiter came up at that moment and Ambrose gave his order. Then Stanhope said:

"And is it permissible to ask if you are pursuing your line of work at the present moment?"

"It has brought me to London – yes. At the actual moment, well, I feel inclined to take advantage of the coincidence."

"Yes? I suppose it's this horrible affair – about poor Hatton?"

The detective-sergeant nodded.

"And you want to pick my brains, eh? But your superintendent did that yesterday."

"Up to a point. But I daresay your brains contain other matter for picking!"

"I told you both all I knew of what took place."

"Yes, you did. But I want to get farther back than that. This is a very puzzling case, Mr. Stanhope. I've only had a few hours' work upon it, but the farther I go, the more I feel mystified."

Stanhope took a pull or two at his pipe, and then said:

"I suppose I ought not to ask if you suspect any particular person of having stabbed Hatton?"

"You may certainly ask, but my reply must be a professional one. It doesn't always do to suspect a particular person in the first stages of investigation. I have to work with an unbiased mind – otherwise I should get the facts distorted. A murder case is a most serious proposition, Mr. Stanhope. It means another human life. Now, if you concentrate on some person who may, all the time, be innocent, you are involving two distinct dangers – first, the danger of, unconsciously perhaps, making the facts suit that person, and secondly, ignoring any inference that those facts really apply to someone else. And you may end in letting the actual criminal escape and hanging the wrong man."

"You interest me greatly," replied Stanhope, "and, if I may say so, you enhance any opinions I may have had of the psychology of police methods – not that I know much about the police. But, you know, you give me the impression – by the very evasiveness of what you say – that there is some particular person, in this case, whom you are tempted to suspect."

Ambrose poured himself out a glass of wine from the small flask of Chianti he had ordered, and laughed.

"As to that," he replied, "I might easily suspect any of the members of your Consultative Committee – you included."

"What!" And the little man started.

"Quite easily! One of you, knowing that Mr. Hatton would be alone, might have returned to the college, say about half-past one, committed the murder, got down the staircase before those two workmen returned, and remained within the college precincts until the rest of the committee came back."

"By George!" exclaimed Stanhope. "Please, sir, it wasn't me, sir! I've got an alibi!"

"I daresay you all have," said Ambrose, "but I'm only showing you how easily and naturally one may have suspicions. But – now that we've met – I want to ask you one or two questions. I'm curious to know why Mr. Hatton brought his luncheon with him yesterday and remained alone in that room."

"He said he had letters to write, and – "

"Yes, you told us that. But, you see, he hadn't written any letters – or even begun one, that we could see. Now, did he know beforehand that the room would be vacant – I mean, that Mr. Henlow would not be in residence?"

"Let me think! Yes – yes, I suppose he did. As a matter of fact Henlow told us at our meeting last month that he'd probably be abroad on his holiday when we met again. But, you know, even if Henlow had been in residence he wouldn't have been in his rooms during our luncheon interval."

"Why not?"

"Because he never had his meals there – except tea."

"I see! Then, anyhow, Hatton could have calculated on remaining there – undisturbed?"

"Certainly."

"Now I'm wondering if he had made an appointment with anyone. Tell me, Mr. Stanhope – he was interested in the design for a stained-glass window you were considering at your meeting yesterday, wasn't he?"

"Old Finmere's detestable, abominable, out-of-drawing memorial to his late missus?" spat out the little artist. "Interested, you ask! He loathed the beastly thing as much as the rest of us. He'd had a row with old Finmere already about it."

"It was not likely that he'd ask Mr. Finmere to come and talk it over with him yesterday – or that Finmere had said he was coming?"

"Of course not. Hatton would have told us. He may have had an appointment, as you suggest, but if he had it was nothing to do with the business of the committee – or he'd have said so."

Ambrose nodded, but said nothing. He went on with his meal for a minute or two, and then remarked:

"I take it you knew Mr. Hatton very intimately, Mr. Stanhope?"

"No, I didn't. We were interested, more or less, in kindred subjects – that was all. Why do you ask?"

"It might help me considerably if I could find out as many details as possible about Mr. Hatton – his habits, and, more particularly, his associates."

"There I can't help you, I'm afraid. But his sister – "

"Yes. I've already seen her. But one sometimes finds that a man's closest friends really know more about him than his relations."

"Well, then, I'd advise you to go and see Dr. Blake – the Professor of Divinity. He would know more about Hatton than anyone else. They've been lifelong friends – from their schooldays."

The detective-sergeant remembered that Miss Hatton had told him her brother was a close friend of the professor, and made up his mind to see Dr. Blake as soon as possible.

Stanhope finished his coffee, knocked the ashes out of his pipe, got up, and reached for his hat.

"Nothing more you want to ask me?"

"No. You've received a notice to attend the inquest tomorrow?"

"I'll be there."

"Oh – one more question. You don't happen to know if Hatton brought a late edition of Monday night's *Evening Gazette* to your meeting?"

"I can answer that. No, he certainly didn't. He hadn't had time to read the morning paper before he came to the meeting, and just before we began business he asked me to let him look at the *Mail* I had with me. He wanted to see the cricket scores in the test match."

"And they, of course, would have been in the evening paper. Thank you, Mr. Stanhope!"

VII

DR. BLAKE, one of the divinity professors of the University, was a tall, dark, austere-looking man with a reputation for profound scholarship. At first sight he struck one as being dry and precise, and, indeed, his books and lectures came under the category of those adjectives.

He had a broad, wrinkled forehead, heavy eyebrows, a large, Roman nose, and a firm, uncompromising-looking mouth. Only, occasionally, the corners of his mouth curled slightly, but with a sure indication that somewhere or other beneath his rather rigid appearance there was a sense of humour.

He was orderly and methodical to a degree. One of his intimate friends, a fellow don who knew him well enough to chaff him, had once sent him for a Christmas present a T-square, with an explanatory letter pointing out that he would find it useful in arranging his books, papers, and other impedimenta, on his study table. For everything on that table was mathematical, parallel and rectangular. If anyone sitting there with him casually took up a book or a ruler or a pen and then laid it down carelessly or askew, Dr. Blake at once altered its position and it became parallel with some other object accordingly.

He had pushed back his chair a little from this table at which he was seated, and was regarding a visiting card which the servant had brought in on a tray.

"Detective-Sergeant Ambrose."

"Very well," he said. "Ask him to come in."

He fixed the sergeant with his piercing dark eyes and, before the latter could utter a word of explanation, said:

"Are you any relation to the Ambrose who used to be Vicar of Derringford?"

"I am his son."

"I thought you were. I could see the resemblance. Also I had heard that a son of his had become a policeman. I knew your father, Mr. Ambrose – years ago. So you didn't follow in his steps?"

"No, sir. He would have liked me to take Orders – but I couldn't see my way."

"Quite right. No man should seek ordination unless he has a distinct call. And now" – he glanced at the card again – "you're a detective, I see. Very interesting! I suppose you go about in all sorts of disguises – ferreting out criminals?"

Ambrose laughed.

"I've never disguised myself in my life, sir," he replied, "except in amateur theatricals. It's mostly in books that detectives assume different characters – and I don't think I could hide my identity by artificial means."

"Oh, yes, you could!" retorted the professor, with the air of a man who was not accustomed to be contradicted. "Look at me, now!"

Ambrose was anxious to get to the point of his visit. But Dr. Blake was not the man to be interrupted. Those who knew him were well aware that if he granted an audience he took control of it.

So, in the force of the professor's compelling personality, Ambrose obeyed meekly – and looked at him accordingly. Dr. Blake went on:

"Do you think that I could easily disguise my appearance?" he asked.

Ambrose smiled, in spite of himself – those heavy eyebrows – that broad forehead – that big nose – that firm-set mouth!

"No – I don't," he replied, candidly.

"That's just where you're wrong, young man," said the professor, triumphantly, "because I've put it to the test."

Perhaps it was that very slight curl at the corners of Dr. Blake's mouth that encouraged Ambrose to ask:

"In ferretting out criminals, sir?"

"No. I was not trespassing on your preserves – and it happened quite inadvertently. I'll tell you.

In the summer of last year I was staying in Cromer. I was suffering from slight eye strain and I bought a pair of sun spectacles with horn rims and dark glasses. On my holidays I do not always affect clerical attire in its strictest sense – that is to say, I sometimes discard what is vulgarly known as the 'dog-collar' and wear an ordinary soft one with a dark tie. Also, whereas I invariably wear the old-fashioned round clerical hat while in residence here, I made use of a Panama at Cromer. Now, observe, young man" – the professor was slipping into his lecturing style – "a pair of glasses; a collar and tie; and a straw hat. That was all. Yet, the very first morning I made use of them I passed, on the parade, two of my fellow guests at the hotel where I was staying, and with whom I had struck an acquaintance, who looked at me but evidently did not recognise me. I was interested enough to put my disguise further to the test, and I soon had the opportunity. For, shortly after, I met, face to face, a man with whom I was very well acquainted indeed. He looked at me. I made no sign of recognition – and he passed me by. The next day I sat on the same seat with him for nearly half an hour – but he took no notice. The third day I met him again – and took off my hat and glasses. Only then did he recognise me – a man, as I say, I knew quite well. Now, you see, the identity of a man is more or less associated with his clothes. It's a question of psychology. People who know me have, in their subconscious minds, an image of a face without spectacles, a clerical collar, and a round black hat. Any variation in this sub-conscious expression – but, dear me, I must not go on with this – though you encouraged me, you know. Now, Mr. Ambrose – you haven't come here to listen to me talking on the psychology of disguises. What have you come about?"

"I came to see if you can give me any information with regard to a very serious case I am investigating – the murder of Mr. Hatton, at St. Oswald's College, yesterday."

"Poor Hatton! It was a terrible shock to me when I heard about it yesterday. He was one of my closest friends. But I know nothing about this horrible tragedy. I fear I can be of no help to you."

"It is just because he was an intimate friend of yours that you may be able to help me, sir. I am only beginning to investigate, and, so far, though certain facts have come to hand, I am by no means satisfied that they will lead to any certainty. A crime like this, meditated or unpremeditated, must have some very strong motive at the bottom of it – and I want to find a motive. Now, sir, knowing Mr. Hatton very intimately as you did, have you any reason for supposing that he had done anything which might excite hatred or revenge – or jealousy?"

The professor leaned back in his chair and closed his eyes. Presently he said:

"I cannot imagine, such a thing."

"There are secrets in most lives, sir," hazarded the detective-sergeant.

"And if I knew one in Hatton's life – would you have me betray the confidence of a dead friend?"

"Certainly I would – if it meant that justice would be vindicated."

"I don't agree with you there. It might be a secret which would not do justice to the memory of the departed – de mortuis nil nisi bonum – not that," he went on emphatically, "there was anything of that sort with Hatton. Let me think a minute, young man."

Again he closed his eyes and leaned back in his chair. And then said:

"Though I cannot conceive it possible that Hatton had an enemy, I think, perhaps, I ought to tell you something. Though, if possible, I would ask you to keep it to yourself."

"If I can, sir – but there may be reasons – "

"Yes, I know. It isn't anything derogatory to poor Hatton, but he would not have cared to have had it talked about. I wonder whether you are sufficiently acquainted with human nature to know that few of us are satisfied with our avowed occupations. Hence our by-paths, which we call our hobbies. Sometimes a man makes his mark more by his hobby than by his profession. Your own father, if I may say so, was better known as a rose grower than as a preacher. When I lecture on St. Luke I point out to my class that though he was a physician it was his literary hobby which has handed him down to posterity – and that none of his prescriptions are preserved or would be worth very much if they were. And I sometimes wonder if, after my death, my collection of miniatures may have a place of honour in the museum to which I shall bequeath them, while my theological books won't fetch twopence a volume on a second-hand bookstall. Well, now, take poor Hatton. He was a great authority on ecclesiastical architecture. If he hadn't had good private means he'd soon have made money by practising as an architect. But, all the time, he had a hobby – and I suppose I'm the only man who knows what it was. In fact, he told me so."

"What was it?"

"Your trade, Mr. Ambrose. The solution of crimes."

"A detective?" exclaimed Ambrose, a little startled.

"No, not exactly a detective – though he might, perhaps, have made a very good one. But he was deeply interested in crime just as a *raison d'etre* for setting up a puzzle and trying to solve it. Theoretically, he read detective stories, but never straight through to a conclusion. If the conclusion were obvious, he threw the book down; if, on the other hand, he found a difficult problem in a story, he set himself to solve it. Simply mental recreation, Mr. Ambrose. One man finds it in chess, Hatton found it in crime.

"But, quite apart from books, Hatton loved an actual crime – that is, if there was a mystery in it. In such a case he studied the newspapers and worked out matters in theory – even jotting his theories down in notebooks, though I never saw them. It is this particular phase of Hatton's mind which set me thinking when you asked me just now if he might have made an enemy of anyone – though, as I said, I cannot conceive it possible."

"All the same, would you mind telling me why your suggestion entered your mind?"

"I will tell you, yes. Because there was one occasion when Hatton really did solve a crime. I mean when he was the cause of actually bringing a criminal to justice."

"This is very interesting, sir."

"Have you ever heard of the Silverton Court burglary case?"

"Why, yes. Though we had nothing to do with it – it took place in another county. Scotland Yard was called in and ran the quarry to earth."

"Scotland Yard did no such thing, young man. It was Hatton. There were very full newspaper reports of the affair – and he studied them closely. Also, he seems to have tried to satisfy his curiosity in other ways. He was spending a week or two at Britwood at the time – a seaside place near Silverton Court, and he studied the actual neighbourhood. Well, one evening I was dining with him and after dinner we were smoking in his study and he produced a few pages of manuscript and said that, at the risk of boring me, he'd read me his conclusions on this Silverton Court affair. But it didn't bore me. It was so lucid, so absolutely logical, that I was deeply interested, and I ended by telling him he ought to communicate his theory to the authorities. At first he wouldn't hear of it – said he'd only worked it out for his own amusement and that the last thing he worked for was publicity. But I invoked him again, on the basis of one's duty to society, and at last, rather reluctantly, he said he would type it and send it anonymously to the Chief Commissioner at Scotland Yard, but that was as far as he would go. Well, he did so, and it was quite obvious to us both in the ensuing arrest and trial that Scotland Yard had accepted his suggestions."

"If I remember rightly it was a fellow named Blaythwaite – one of the guests staying in the house at the time of the robbery – and he got three years."

"He got three years! Exactly. Now, supposing – what seems impossible – that this Blaythwaite had got to know that, in some way or other, Hatton was responsible for his conviction – but – of course, it's out of the question. The three years are not up yet, and – "

"Yes, but," broke in Ambrose, "Blaythwaite might be out of prison on leave by this time – if he'd earned his good conduct marks."

"Ah! I never thought of that!"

"I shall have to make inquiries – anyhow. As you say, sir, it seems impossible, but there may be something in it. I'm greatly obliged to you, sir, for telling me all this. Is there anything else you think I ought to know?"

"Well, now – I don't know that it would help you – but perhaps I'd better mention it. Poor Hatton has been engaged recently on trying to solve another problem – one that concerns myself. By the way, it's a problem, too, in which you ought to be interested, for the police here know about it – the loss of my 'Cosway.'"

"Ah – yes. I know exactly what you mean. But I have not been personally engaged upon it – two of our men – and the superintendent – have it in hand."

"And don't seem to have done much!" retorted the professor, dryly. "And my Cosway, young man, is only one incident in a series – extending over nearly two years, all small objects, but of intrinsic value. Since this miniature of mine was taken – about three months ago – there was that Corot – cut clean out of its frame in the Provost of Malvern's dining-room. What's become of them is a problem in itself, for they are not saleable – openly. But to get back to Hatton. He was profoundly interested in the loss of my Cosway – just the sort of mystery he loved. He almost grew to be a bother – he dropped in so often to ask me questions. About ten days ago he told me he believed he had a faint vestige of a clue and asked me to let him have a look at the padlock with which the case containing the miniatures was fastened – look here – I'd like to show you."

Dr. Blake got up from his seat and crossed the room. The detective-sergeant followed him. In a corner stood a small Corean chest, of polished wood, clamped with ornamental brass.

"I keep the gems of my collection here," he said. "Oh, no – I don't trust to those clumsy Corean locks, and, in fact, I don't use them at all. My fastening is this padlock – a letter lock, you observe. Eight small revolving cylinders with a series of eight letters on each. Do you know anything about permutation of numbers?"

"I know something about bell ringing," said Ambrose with a laugh. "I learnt ringing in my father's parish. So I know that there are five thousand and forty combinations of letters in this lock of yours."

"Quite right! So it is not likely that mere guesswork would give you the right one. Now, this is not the padlock which was on the chest when my Cosway was taken. This is a new lock put on the stable door after the horse was stolen, so to speak. And the makers, when I purchased it, gave me the word which opens it, and assured me there was not, and never would be, a duplicate. And I am the only person who knows that word. No – I'm not going to let even a policeman see it. You may look, but you won't find out anything."

Carefully shielding, with the fingers of one hand, the top of the lock, he revolved the cylinders till he had made the necessary adjustment. In a few moments he slid it into two parts, and then rapidly shifted the cylinders once more.

"There! You couldn't see the word, eh?"

"No."

The professor chuckled.

"I'm a very careful man," he observed, "and I've always taken particular care in opening this case when anyone else is near. I've never even let my dearest friends – or even my wife and daughter – catch a glimpse of my password. And yet – with all my precautions – that Cosway went! It was the only one missing – look!"

And he opened the chest. It was full of miniatures of all kinds.

"This particular one," he went on, "was a gold snuff box with Cosway's work on it – an exquisite design. The box itself was of considerable value, not simply because of the intrinsic worth of the gold – which was beautifully chased – but on account of its historical associations. Connoisseurs had very little doubt that it was originally in the possession of the Regent, and was given by him to Beau Brummel before that precious pair fell out. The sale of the snuff box among Brummel's goods is authenticated. The miniature was one of Cosway's masterpieces, probably the finest ever executed by that great artist. Of course, though in my private collection, it was well known to the outer world – well known, too, that it was in my possession.

"But I must not take up your time with my hobby," went on Dr. Blake. "So I will get back to what I was telling you about Hatton. He asked, as I said, to see the old padlock – another eight-letter combination. Here it is."

He had gone back to his table and opened a drawer in it, producing a similar padlock to the one with which the Corean chest was fitted, but a trifle smaller.

"Well, Hatton examined it very closely – first asking me to give him the combination – which I did. As I was not going to use the padlock again there was no longer any reason for concealment. After looking at the thing for a minute or two he said to me, 'Blake – I have a theory. It's a very far-fetched one, but I'm going to follow it up.' I asked him to tell me what it was, but he refused. 'I may most likely be wrong,' he said, 'and if I am I would not care to let anyone know what I have in mind.' There! That was all. I don't for a moment suppose it has anything to do with this horrible murder, but you asked me to tell you what I knew about Hatton."

"I'm glad you told me this, sir. I can't, of course, deduce anything from it, but I shall take it into consideration. The possibility arises that in pursuing this problem of the theft of your miniature he may have, unconsciously perhaps, trod upon dangerous ground. There must have been some strong motive for taking his life, and, sometimes, a motive forms the central basis of an investigation."

Dr. Blake had gone back to the Corean chest, and was adjusting the fastening once more.

"There!" he exclaimed, "it seems impossible that anyone but myself could open that lock – unless he spent many hours trying every combination which exists!"

The detective-sergeant smiled.

"Will you allow me to try?" he asked.

The professor wheeled round sharply.

"You!" he cried. "You can't possibly know – "

"May I try?"

Dr. Blake laughed.

"Certainly – but I can't see – go on, then."

He stepped back from the chest. Ambrose advanced, stooped over it, and slowly began turning the eight cylindrical rings of the padlock.

In about three minutes he stood up and held out his open palm towards Dr. Blake. The padlock lay thereon – in two parts.

"How on earth!" cried the astounded professor. "Are you a new Houdini, Mr. Ambrose? How could you possibly have guessed?"

"I find guesswork particularly dangerous in my profession, sir, and I try to avoid it. I didn't guess. I knew."

"But you couldn't know. I took care of that when I set the combination. You never saw the word."

"You must forgive me, sir. I am constantly practising the art of observation, especially in little things. When you told me, as you began to set the combination, that you were not going to let me see it, you threw out a challenge which put me, professionally, on my mettle. It's quite true that you shielded the actual word from my view, but your fingers didn't quite cover the whole of the padlock, and I was able to read a line of letters below them. I memorised those letters – 'B.L.T.E.F.T.C.U.' Now, I at once realised that if I could get that combination in line in one part of the cylinder, I should have the actual word in another part, and, by turning the cylinder, I should soon be able to cover the correct alignment and slip the lock. It took me a little longer than I thought, because there are two 'B's' on the first ring and two 'F's' on the fifth and, in my first effort, I got them both in the wrong places. But, when I turned the cylinder to see the other seven combinations, there was only one of them which at all resembled a word – and that was 'JUTSLAND.' It was, then, only a matter of a crossword puzzle, so to speak, to find the real word 'OUTSTAND.' All very simple, sir – but going to prove, what I was thinking all the time, that you can't really depend on letter locks."

"I think you chose your profession advisedly, young man," replied the professor, "and you ought to succeed in it. But your experiment proves something else – it proves me to be a fool!"

"Oh, I wouldn't say that, sir."

"Of course you wouldn't. I'm not in the habit of being called a fool to my face – even by undergraduates. What I mean is that if you solved the combination so easily someone else with equally sharp brains may have done so, too."

"You will have to try to remember the various people who saw you open the chest – with the other padlock."

"How can you expect me to do that?" exclaimed the professor testily. "I've shown my collection to scores of people – intimate friends, fellow collectors, and even strangers who have called upon me – Americans, some of them. I can't call them all to mind. No! But I shall get a lock and key padlock – this very day. I run no more risks."

"I think you are wise, sir" – he got up to go – "and thank you very much for giving me your time and help."

The professor shook hands with him.

"I'm only too glad if I've been of any use to you. First because you're your father's son, and secondly because I'd do anything in my power to help to bring the villain who killed my poor friend to a conviction. Come again if you think I can help you farther – and, give me your private address. If I hear of anything I'll communicate with you direct. I haven't a great opinion of your fellow policemen, young man, for they've done nothing in the way of recovering my Cosway. But you seem to have your wits about you. You ought to get on. Goodbye!"

VIII

A TAXI pulled up at the gateway of St. Oswald's College. The porter, who was just outside his lodge, came forward and took the two suitcases belonging to the occupant, who got out.

"Williams had my postcard?"

"Yes, sir, this morning. He went at once to the police station to get the key of your room – you'll find everything ready for you."

"The police station? Oh, yes – I begin to understand. I suppose the police kept the key. What a terrible affair! I was abroad when it happened and did not see an English newspaper for a day or two later. I don't know the full details even now. It gave me a shock."

"It gave us all a shock, sir. Such a thing has never happened in the college before. . . . I'll send Williams up with your things, sir."

"Tell him to bring me tea first. These can wait."

"Very good, sir."

Mr. Sidney Henlow walked slowly through the two quads and ascended the staircase to his rooms. He was a man of about fifty, with iron-grey hair, rather scanty over the temples, and clean-shaven face, thin and spare. He stooped slightly, and had the air of an "indoor man." His expression, which was intellectual, had a solemn touch about it and, indeed, Henlow was known among his friends in the university as a scholar, with very little sense of humour. Someone had once referred to him as resembling an astringent, so dry was his manner and conversation, and from that time he was often referred to as "Stringy Henlow."

There was a cheerful fire burning in his room. He glanced round it with the air of a man glad to get back to intimate surroundings. Slowly he divested himself of his overcoat and sat down in one of the armchairs beside the fire, stretching out his hands to warm them at the blaze, for the day was a damp, chill autumn one. In a few minutes Williams came in, carrying a tray bearing on it tea, hot buttered toast, and cake.

"Ah, Williams! How are you?"

"Quite all right, sir, thank you. Glad to see you back, sir. I hope you're well, sir?"

And he set the tray on the table.

"I'm well, Williams, but I'm worried. I can't bear to think of this dreadful tragedy taking place in my room."

"Dreadful indeed, sir. I can't get it out of my head either – shall I pour you out a cup of tea, sir?"

Henlow nodded. Williams handed him tea and toast, and went on:

"I was with poor Mr. Hatton, sir, only just before it took place. I little thought he would have been sitting in that very chair you're in now, not more than an hour and a half afterwards, done to death by a murderer."

Henlow gave an involuntary shiver.

"In this chair, was he?"

"He was, sir. Mr. Kershaw and Mr. Stanhope found him there when they came back from their lunch."

"Tell me all about it, Williams. I don't know more than I've seen in the newspapers."

"No, sir, of course not. You was in Geneva at the time –"

Williams, nothing loath, stood there, recounting all that had taken place. Henlow went on with his tea, now and then interposing a question or remark. From time to time Williams, without pausing in his narrative, passed the toast or the cake.

"I suppose the police made a thorough search, Williams – at the time?"

"They did, sir. The superintendent went everywhere – into the room across the landing – I had to bring him the key – and in your bedroom here – even looking into the wardrobe, sir – so he said. And all of us in the college were cross-questioned and had to account for our movements. I tell you, sir, that superintendent put the wind up me. He hinted that as I'd been the last person who saw Mr. Hatton alive I might have murdered him myself. As if I'd do such a thing, sir. But my belief is – and there's others in the college who think the same – that the police wasted their time here. The man as done the deed wasn't here then, sir, and it was no use looking for him. Why, one of the super's men – a detective-sergeant – spent a couple of hours in these rooms, all by himself, the next morning. Silly, I call it. By the way, sir, when I went to fetch the key this morning – for they wouldn't let me keep it – the superintendent asked me to let him know when you was back. He said he'd like to see you."

"That's quite natural, Williams. Of course he would. You go and telephone to him at once and say he can come as soon as he likes. I shan't be going out before dinner."

"Very good, sir."

Henlow slowly finished his tea, lighted a cigarette, and leaned back in his chair. Williams appeared again presently, bringing in the suitcases. And proceeded to remove the tea tray.

"I've 'phoned to the superintendent, sir, and he says he's coming to see you at once."

"All right, Williams. He knows his way up here, I suppose?"

"He ought to, sir."

Williams went out. Henlow crossed the room and unlocked a cigar cabinet, taking a box from it and putting it on the table. Then he sat down again and waited. In a few minutes there was a knock at the door.

"Come in – ah, good evening, superintendent. Take a seat, won't you?"

"I'm sorry to disturb you, sir, but I was anxious to see you as soon as you returned."

"I quite understand. Won't you have a cigar?" and he passed the box. "I'm sorry I've nothing to offer you to drink."

"Thank you, sir – but I never take any."

He lighted his cigar. For some minutes the two men discussed the murder, Henlow asking occasional questions. Then he said:

"And may I ask if you are making any progress in tracking down the murderer?"

"We are doing our best, sir. But at present I'm not in a position to discuss that point at any length."

"I read a brief account of the inquest – in a daily paper. But they didn't seem to have arrived at anything."

"They wouldn't, sir. The opening proceedings were purely formal and the inquest was adjourned. I called no witnesses."

"Have you witnesses, then?"

The superintendent evaded the question.

"I wish I had a witness to the actual murder," he said grimly, "but that rarely happens! Now, Mr. Henlow, I've a few questions I should like to ask you – if you don't mind."

"Certainly."

"Did Mr. Hatton know that you would be away when the committee met on this particular occasion?"

"He probably thought I should. I mentioned, at the previous meeting, that, in all probability, I should be abroad."

"Then there was, really, no necessity for you to write from Geneva to the secretary – Mr. Pennington – telling him this room was available, as usual?"

"No necessity, no! But Pennington is a very precise fellow – he likes to have everything in writing."

"I see. Have you ever known any of the committee bring their luncheon with them?"

"Never."

"And, I understand, you never lunched in this room."

"No."

"So that Mr. Hatton would naturally gather that he would have the room to himself during the luncheon hour?"

"Quite a reasonable inference."

"You knew Mr. Hatton well, of course?"

"Yes, certainly."

"You can't suggest any reason for anyone having a grudge against him?"

"Not in the least."

"Or say any reason why anyone finding him in this room should have resented his presence?"

Henlow smiled.

"I can only imagine a burglar," he replied. "Not that any burglar would have found it worth his while to ransack my rooms. I have nothing of value here – except a few rare books." And he pointed to the bookcase.

The superintendent had taken out his notebook and was jotting down Henlow's replies to his questions. He suddenly paused, his pencil held in mid-air. Rare books! Ambrose had told him of his interview with Dr. Blake and how the professor had said that Hatton was interested in the series of thefts of small, but highly valuable articles, extending over a period of nearly two years. He remembered, also, that – among these articles – the Warmingham Missal had been taken. A rare book! And there followed in his mind the suggestion that others, besides the members of the committee, might have known that Henlow's rooms were unoccupied and unlocked during the luncheon hour on the first Tuesday in the month.

"Are any of them missing?" he rapped out, sharply. So sharply that Henlow was taken aback.

"Any missing?" he repeated. "Oh, you mean my books?"

"Yes, sir. Do you mind looking?"

Henlow got up and walked slowly to the bookcase. He stood there, reaching up to upper shelves, stooping to examine lower ones. He laid his finger on certain books, checking them carefully.

"No," he said, at length, "they are all there. Why did you imagine any of them might be missing?"

The superintendent shrugged his shoulders.

"You, yourself, suggested a possible burglar," he replied, "or," he added, with a slight smile, "technically speaking, I should say housebreaker! Burglars are gentlemen who work after nine p.m."

Henlow returned to his chair, a puzzled look on his face. The superintendent looked at his notebook and frowned. He was a cautious man, and was rapidly calculating how far he could take Sidney Henlow into his confidence. He did not wish, at that juncture, to drag in Finmere's name, though he knew, sooner or later, Finmere's visit was bound to leak out. The vicar of Little Marpleton knew Fimmere was going to Henlow's rooms, Hastings, the artist, knew he had been there and the insurance clerk, Wilkins, though he did not as yet know it was Finmere, had actually seen the latter – in the room. But the superintendent was particularly anxious that the press should get no inkling of this at present.

At the same time he wanted more information from Henlow. Henlow was the actual occupier of the rooms and might be in a position to know more than anybody else as regards one particular point. The superintendent knew perfectly well that if Finmere had committed the crime he had probably left the college before one thirty-five, and so escaped observation. But he shared Ambrose's hesitancy with regard to fixing the crime on Finmere and neglecting any other possibility. If Finmere left the college unobserved before one thirty-five, someone else might have come in afterwards, also unobserved and before one thirty-five. The question was, how could such a person have got out?

He determined to risk a little without mentioning names.

"Mr. Henlow," he said, at length. "What I am going to say now I must ask you to treat as confidential – at least for the present."

"I quite understand."

"There are great difficulties in this case, and they rest, partly, on the question of time. We know the murder must have been committed between a quarter past one and half-past two. We also know that the porter's vigilance was relaxed from one o'clock for thirty-five minutes. Now your servant, Williams, was with Mr. Hatton in this room at a few minutes after one."

"So he told me just now. He was the last person, he said, to see poor Hatton alive."

"Couldn't have been!" retorted the superintendent.

"Why?"

"The man who killed him was the last person to see him alive, sir."

"Yes, yes, I see. Of course he was. Well?"

"Now we happen to know that a man came into this room shortly after Williams had left it."

"Why – of course – the murderer?"

"Maybe – and maybe not," replied the superintendent, dryly; "anyhow, he was seen to come in."

"Seen to come in?" ejaculated Henlow. "But if that's the case" – he broke off – "who saw him?"

"That I prefer not to tell you at present. But we have his description – and we shall run him down right enough."

"What was his description?"

"That – again, I won't say, sir. But I have my reasons for saying that, though we have his description and know he was here with Mr. Hatton, we are not at all satisfied in our minds that he really committed the crime. If he did, he probably got away before one thirty-five. If he didn't – and there are reasons for conjecturing that Mr. Hatton was killed a little later – then the murderer must have left these rooms before half-past two. And we know he didn't leave after two, because the two workmen at the bottom of the stairs would have seen him."

"I should imagine from what you and Williams have told me, that it is quite obvious that he left before the workmen came back. Does not the finding of my paper-knife at the foot of the stairs prove that?"

"Then, if he did, where did he go to?" said the superintendent. "He didn't leave the college. The porter would have seen him."

"Probably he hid somewhere – in the college precincts, and made his escape later on."

The superintendent shook his head.

"We made a thorough search. I had two of my men up from the station to do that. That won't do, sir. And that brings me to my question. You are, naturally, better acquainted with these rooms than anyone else: you occupy them. Now, Mr. Henlow, is there any way by which a man could get from here out of the college without going down the staircase, through the two quads, and out at the gateway? More especially without going down the staircase?"

"Without going down the staircase?" echoed Henlow, and began to stroke his chin thoughtfully. "Let me see – he couldn't get up to the roof, that's out of the question – and you say that he left before half-past two?"

"Must have done. There's no other solution."

"You looked in the room across the landing?"

"Of course we did, sir. It was locked, and Williams had the only key."

"Humph!" Henlow got up and walked to and fro, thinking. Then he went into the bay of the oriel window – opened it, and looked out.

"I have heard," he said, "that a former occupant of these rooms – an undergraduate who was gated for a fortnight – once hung a rope out of this window and got out – and in. It might even be possible for a younger man than I am to let himself drop – without a rope. I wouldn't care to try it myself!"

The superintendent smiled.

"We thought of that, sir. But it was in the middle of the day, and the street was full of people. We should very soon have heard about it!"

"Then I know of no other way. I suppose you searched my rooms carefully?"

"We did, sir – immediately after the murder, and my detective-sergeant spent some time here the following day."

"And you found nothing? No clue that would give you any hint – ?"

The superintendent shook his head. He was not going to mention the newspaper or the trivial array of articles collected by Ambrose. They, at all events, had nothing to do with the question he had asked Henlow. He threw the stump of his cigar into the fire.

"I'm sorry to have troubled you, sir. And I'm sorry, too, for all the inconvenience you have been put to in having your room made the scene of a crime."

"No inconvenience at all. I was out of it, you see. But I deeply regret the loss of a colleague, and my sympathies are not for myself, but for his poor, unfortunate sister. She was devoted to him."

"Poor lady!" exclaimed the superintendent. "She has taken it very bravely – outwardly. A terrible ordeal, too, for her – the inquest. We were all sorry for her."

"I'm sure you were! I must get out to Little Marpleton and see her tomorrow – goodnight, superintendent."

Mr. Henlow, after the superintendent had gone, took a book from the bookcase, lighted his pipe, and settled himself comfortably in the armchair which had so recently held the body of his dead friend. There was, evidently, nothing superstitious in his constitution. Presently Williams tapped at the door, and came in.

"Would you like me to unpack your suitcases, sir?"

Without taking his eyes from his book, Mr. Henlow fumbled in his waistcoat pocket and produced a key.

"The larger one, Williams. The other can wait."

And went on reading. He could hear Williams moving about in the bedroom – unpacking, and arranging his clothes.

Williams came out of the bedroom. Henlow glanced up from his book.

"What are you doing with those shoes? I was going to wear them presently – they don't want cleaning."

"This is not the pair I took out of your suitcase, sir. It's one of those you left behind. I've just noticed that one of the laces is missing, and I'm taking them to put in a new pair – I keep a stock of laces, sir."

"Oh, yes. I see."

Henlow did not, at first, recommence reading. A puzzled expression crept over his face. He forgot to draw at his pipe. It went out.

IX

CHIEF-INSPECTOR FERGUSON of the C.I.D. sat at his desk in his office in Scotland Yard, studying a voluminous typewritten report. He was a tall, heavy-looking man, with fair hair and moustache. He looked as if he took life easily. In a manner of speaking he did take life easily, that is to say that although he put in, with the rest of his colleagues, an enormous amount of hard work, nothing seemed to disturb his habitual good nature and equanimity. He wore a perpetual smile, as if secretly amused by some joke which he was keeping to himself. It was a deceptive smile, as more than one gentleman enjoying the law's free hospitality had good reason to know, for Ferguson was never more dangerous to the criminal than when he was apparently beaming upon him with loving kindness in his heart.

In the "Yard," Chief-Inspector Ferguson had a reputation for a perfectly uncanny memory where dates were concerned. He had a habit of quoting months and days – even hours – as if he were an animated diary, and was never known to have referred to a notebook or almanac when a particular date from the past had to be dug up.

A clerk came into his office and gave him a card. Ferguson looked at it.

"Oh, Ambrose – from Exbridge. All right, I can see him now. Tell him to come in – Good-morning, sergeant. We've met before, haven't we? You came to see me on the thirteenth of October last year. Well, what's the news from Exbridge? Have you come to ask the Yard to step in and solve that murder case for you?"

Ambrose laughed.

"That's a matter for my chief to decide, inspector. And I hope he's not going to do it – yet, at anyrate."

"Just like you country bumpkins. You go and muddle things first and then send for us when the mess wants clearing up."

"Anyhow it's about the murder I've come to see you," replied Ambrose. "I won't confess I'm stumped – but I am a bit puzzled."

"Never be puzzled, my friend," beamed the inspector. "It's a bad habit, and it doesn't help. Nothing, in human nature, is really a puzzle – what seems so only implies ignorance of it. Well, what is it?"

"I believe you were engaged on a case of burglary – at a place called Silverton Court, some time ago."

"Night of July the fifteenth, nineteen twenty-nine," answered the inspector promptly. "What about it?"

"And you got your man?"

"Blaythwaite – yes. A clever dog, but a bad hat. Captain Blaythwaite. Public school and university man, too. Well?"

"Sharp bit of work on your part, inspector?" hazarded Ambrose, a twinkle in his eye. "Striking example of the deductive method, the detective novelist would call it."

Ferguson looked at the other – and beamed.

"Now, what are you getting at, sergeant?" he asked. "Why this flattery? You've something behind it."

"There was something behind your investigation, wasn't there?"

"What?"

"An anonymous communication?"

The chief inspector leaned forward in his chair.

"And if there was," he said, "what the devil is it to do with you? What do you know about it?"

"That it was sent to the commissioner here, and that it was written by Mr. Francis Hatton, the man who was murdered at Exbridge last Tuesday."

"Eh – what? How do you know this, sergeant?" Ambrose told him. The inspector was deeply interested.

"So that's who sent us the letter! I've often wondered who it was. All I can say is this corpse of yours must have been a devilish clever fellow! That letter was a masterpiece. I was inclined to put it in the waste-paper basket with a lot of other rubbishy communications at first – his theory seemed so preposterous. But the more I thought it over, the more I saw the cold logic of it – and I followed it up. I don't mind admitting that I caught my bird through it. I should like to have met this fellow Hatton. But how does it fit in with his death?"

"There's just a chance. Blaythwaite may have found out, somehow, that Hatton wrote that letter, and – "

"Revenge?" broke in Ferguson. "I shouldn't think so. Blaythwaite might – and did – risk a stretch of prison, but he wasn't the sort to risk a stretch of his neck. Besides – he was convicted at the Frattenbury Assizes on September the twenty-fourth that year – he couldn't be out yet – not even with the maximum of good conduct marks. I'll make sure."

He seized the telephone receiver on his desk and rang up one of the departments of the building.

"No!" he said, presently, "he's still at Parkhurst. And that's that! You were right to follow up the notion, sergeant, though it wasn't a very likely one. Blaythwaite could hardly get hold of the fact that this chap Hatton put us on his track. We didn't know who the writer of the letter was – let alone mentioning the letter at all, which, of course, we never did. Only Hatton himself and this professor of yours seem to have known. No! It's no good going on that tack."

"I quite see that – especially as Blaythwaite is still in prison."

The inspector wheeled round in his chair.

"Though on second thoughts, that might not have ruled your theory out."

"What do you mean?"

"I mean Blaythwaite's got a wife – who isn't in prison. And I'd back a woman to hatch a revenge before I would a man – even if she takes years over it. I don't suppose there's anything in it, but it's just as well that I should tell you all we know of Blaythwaite and his wife. It may be useful, too, if Blaythwaite tries any games in your county when he comes out."

Again he took up the telephone receiver and gave an order. In a few seconds a clerk came in carrying a small portfolio, and put it down on the inspector's desk.

"Ha!" said the latter, opening it. "Here we are. Mostly information we got after Blaythwaite's arrest. Some of it after his conviction. When we get a bird in our little net we like to know as much as we can about him. May be useful later on. Let's see – I'll give you the gist of it. Hartley James Blaythwaite – educated at Banhurst and Exbridge. Private secretary to Sir Peter Deverell – some time in America – served in France during the Great War – rank of Captain – fair record. Since appears to have tried various occupations – latterly apparently well off. Received in good society. Convicted of theft of Lady Fullinger's pearl necklace and other jewellery while staying with his wife as guests at Silverton Court, near Britwood. Subsequent information points to criminal connections, but nothing proved. No case against his wife, though collusion with above theft suspected.

"After her husband's conviction Mrs. Blaythwaite took a house in Elsworth Road. Hampstead, under her maiden name of Mrs. Harford. Lives there in comfortable circumstances. Under occasional observation, but nothing has transpired. Note – to keep both under observation on Blaythwaite's discharge from prison.

"There!" went on the inspector. "You see we have our suspicions concerning his wife as well as himself. I've put you wise on the chief points, but I can't see it has anything to do with this murder case of yours. It isn't at all likely that either of them got wind of the notion that this fellow Hatton wrote to us about the robbery. Anything more I can do for you?"

"Nothing, thanks."

"Let me know if there is. Well, good luck, sergeant. I hope you'll get your man. It's an interesting case, from what I've read of it. Sort of thing I like to have a hand in – Perhaps I shall!" he added, with a laugh, as the detective-sergeant got up to go.

The latter laughed in return.

"I hope not – for my own reputation," he replied.

For a moment Chief Inspector Ferguson hesitated. Then he said, in a kindly tone of voice:

"I'm an old hand at the game, my lad – and I know how you're feeling. But we don't track criminals simply for the sake of our own reputations – and the success of the police lies more in their team work than in the individual, in spite of the story books. One word more – an unofficial one. I like to see a smart man get on. If ever you want a bit of advice from one who knows the ropes a bit, come and see me – as a friend."

Ambrose was struck by the warm friendly attitude suddenly adopted by the chief inspector. There are times when one feels the need of a confidence which is apart from official restrictions, and Ferguson seemed to offer just such a confidence at that moment. The younger man paused, his hand on the door, ready to depart; then he closed the door again and came back.

"You're very kind," he said. "May I, then, ask you something – as a friend?"

Ferguson motioned him to sit down once more.

"Go ahead," he said.

"Well, it's this way," began Ambrose. "I'm on the track of a man who seems to fit in as the murderer of Mr. Hatton, and against whom there's quite a little pile of evidence. I have a witness who saw this fellow in Hatton's company a very short time – probably only a few minutes – before the murder. I know that he had a knife in his hand when he was with Hatton. I know, also, that he was a very bad tempered man, and that he had what he considered to be a cause for a quarrel with Hatton. I know that he had every opportunity of killing Hatton and escaping from the college unobserved, and that, in fact, he was the only person, apparently, who could have done so within a time-limit that is conclusively fixed. And yet – well – I can't feel certain about it."

"One seldom can be absolutely certain," remarked Ferguson, dryly. "Preponderance of probability is often the furthest one dare venture upon. But you interest me. I'm not barging into your case – this is quite unofficial – give me the details, will you?"

As briefly as possible, Ambrose told him about Finmere's visit to Henlow's rooms, and recounted his interview with the artist, Hastings. The chief inspector listened in silence, but those who knew him well, could they have seen the genial smile beaming upon his face, would have said that he was deeply interested.

"There," said Ambrose, when he had finished, "I'd be glad to have your opinion."

"What does your superintendent think about it?" retorted Ferguson.

"He – and the chief constable – are down on Finmere. They want him, badly."

"H'm! Very natural. You've got to get hold of the fellow, anyhow."

"I know. Of course if he were at home we could detain him."

"Yes. But you've got to charge him definitely if it's a question of extradition. You want my opinion – unofficially? Very well. I'll take the pros and cons. The pros are – a hot-tempered man – unexpectedly finding the fellow he thought had thwarted him most alone – quarrelling with him – a sudden impulse of blind anger – a blow with the weapon he happened to have in his hand – a hasty escape from the scene of crime. But the rest doesn't tally. There's one big con against it, and that's his visit to this artist chap – and what he told him – that he'd been in that room with Hatton and that he was actually using the knife to extract the drawing pins. Only a big fool would have done that. I suppose," he went on, leaning forward suddenly, "you're quite sure Hatton was stabbed with that particular knife? What does your doctor man say about it?"

"He's a cautious fellow," replied Ambrose, "and refuses to say more than that the wound was caused by a sharp-pointed instrument and that this knife might be that instrument."

"What makes him hesitate?"

"He says that the breadth of the wound where the incision took place is slightly more than the width of the knife blade, and that this may be due to a lateral movement when the actual stabbing took place, but that he cannot say so definitely."

"I see. Well, be that as it may, let's try to follow up this fellow Finmere's doings with an open mind. If he did commit the crime you'll find it difficult to prove it. You've only got one witness, and he only saw him momentarily from across the way. The only other evidence is what Finmere told the artist – and that's rather in his favour than otherwise. I don't see that you've enough to go upon to get an extradition warrant, but, at the same time, it is imperative to get hold of Finmere as soon as possible, and not wait for his possible return to England. Suppose he's innocent, and you argue from that that he would have communicated with you. It doesn't follow. He left the country before the affair got into the newspapers, and he's travelling on the Continent. The chances are that he may not have seen an English newspaper. Now you tell me that he was making for Paris first, and that he said he might be going on to Evian-les-Bains?"

"That is so."

"Well, there's no reason to doubt his word if he's innocent, is there? Now I'll tell you what I'll do. I happen to know the commissaire of the district and he owes me a good turn in relation to a case in which I was able to help him. I'll ring him up and ask him to let me know if Finmere puts in an appearance – he's got to register at any hotel he goes to. It'll save you the bother of hunting around for him. Then you'll have to go to Evian-les-Bains – I suppose you can arrange this with your super?"

"Easily."

"Good! As soon as I hear I'll ring you up at Exbridge."

"It's very good of you."

"Not a bit. One thing more – though I dare say you've got it in your mind already – if Finmere isn't your man, then all I can say is you've got to find a devilish clever fellow!"

X

DETECTIVE-SERGEANT AMBROSE, weary with his long train journey, got out at the station at Evian-les-Bains and inquired his way to the Police Bureau.

The commissaire, a genial official, a stout, heavy-looking man, but whose penetrating dark eyes gave the lie to any suspicion of lethargy, looked up from the desk at which he was seated as Ambrose came into the room.

"Ah!" he said. "My good friend Monsieur Fairguson has told me to expect you. Be seated, monsieur. You speak French? Good! We shall the better understand one another."

After a little exchange of compliments the commissaire came to the point.

"This Monsieur Finmere, yes! You will find him at the Lion d'Or, in the face of the lake near the quay. We have observed him since his arrival – but, you understand, not in any official sense. You have not come to ask our professional help, is it not so?"

"That is true, monsieur. But it is good of you to have taken so much trouble."

"Bah! It is nothing! I am charmed to be of any use to Monsieur Fairguson and, through him, to you. But now my little action in your affair comes to an end. I leave it to you, monsieur, to do what you please. But – naturally – there must be no arrest!"

"I quite understand, Monsieur le Commissaire. I have come to ask him to make a voluntary statement, and, if he will, to return to England with me."

The commissaire placed his forefinger on the side of his nose, and laughed.

"Ah, your English ways!" he ejaculated. "They amuse me much. You are so careful, even when dealing with those whom you know are criminals. You caution them, lest they should commit themselves – you treat them all the time as if they were innocent saints. I think I prefer our French methods, monsieur. But we will not argue the point. Where are you staying?"

"I came straight here from the station. I have not yet found an hotel."

The Frenchman's face instantly took on a serious expression.

"Then let me advise you, monsieur. Go to the Belle Vue Hotel in the Rue d'Albion. It is small, I grant you – but the cuisine! Ah! It is of the best. You shall tell the proprietor, Monsieur Charlier, that I sent you there and that he is to command his chef to give you one of his omelettes – and provide a bottle of the Burgundy I had when last I dined there. And I will advise you further. It is late – almost past the hour of dinner. In this affair of yours there is no need for haste – you could not take this Monsieur Finmere back with you before tomorrow. Wait, then, till the morning before you call on him – he shall not run away. Do not spoil the digestion of a good dinner, my friend!"

Ambrose, as he made his way to the Belle Vue, felt inclined to take the commissaire's advice. He was very tired, and he knew that a convenient train to Paris left about midday. So he made up his mind to dine comfortably, have a good night, and interview Finmere as early as possible the next morning.

The Lion d'Or was a large hotel, standing in its own grounds, with a magnificent view of the lake. It was about nine o'clock when Ambrose called. Several of the guests were sitting at small tables on a sheltered terrace in front of the hotel, discussing rolls and coffee. Ambrose inquired of the hall porter if Mr. Finmere was in, and a waiter who was standing near and overheard said that Monsieur Finmere was taking his petit dejeuner on the terrace; he would conduct monsieur to him.

George Wilkins' description rose to the sergeant's mind as he saw a red-faced man, with a white moustache, seated at one of the tables. Finmere looked up.

"Yes. What is it?"

Ambrose introduced himself.

"I've come from Exbridge, sir," he explained, "and I'd be glad if you would give me an interview – on rather an important matter."

"Exbridge, hey?" ejaculated Finmere. "What do you want to see me about?"

Ambrose glanced round at the other guests.

"If you've finished your breakfast, sir," he replied, "could we go somewhere where we can talk in private?"

Finmere looked at him again, very sharply, hesitated a moment, then got up abruptly from his chair, and said:

"Come along!"

Ambrose followed him into the hotel. Finmere led the way to a small smoking-room, which was empty, turned round and shut the door.

"Now!" he exclaimed, "out with it, man! Have you come to arrest me? Because, if you have, I want to see your warrant. And I warn you that it'll have to be in order – extradition and all that sort of thing – and also that I insist on seeing the British vice-consul here before you take any further steps."

The detective-sergeant was somewhat taken aback by this outburst.

"You are making a mistake, Mr. Finmere," he replied, quietly. "There is no question of arrest but I see you know the reason why I am here."

"Of course I do," retorted Finmere, irritably. "I'm not a fool. Though it was only last night that I knew," he added. "It's about that confounded fellow Hatton, I suppose, isn't it?"

Ambrose nodded.

"Quite right, sir. I'm investigating the case."

"The devil you are! And you want to get me to commit myself, hey? Well, you won't!"

"Excuse me, Mr. Finmere, but you are jumping to conclusions rather hastily. I told you I have no warrant to arrest you and I have no charge to make against you. Nor can I compel you to make any statement. But I am going to ask you to help me."

"Warning me first that anything I say will be taken down and – "

"Come, come, sir! Nothing of the kind! But you know that a terrible murder has been committed, and I know that you were with Hatton immediately before it took place."

"So you think I killed him, hey?"

"I never suggested such a thing. Come, Mr. Finmere, be reasonable! I'm not accusing you of the crime. I'm only doing my duty in the interests of justice. You must see that your position calls for an explanation – in your own interests."

The testy old squire was calming down a little under the suave demeanour of the detective-sergeant. But his tone was still one of irritation as he replied:

"What I object to is coercion. I tell you I only knew of the miserable affair last night. Do you suppose I should have hidden myself here and taken no steps? Of course not. I was only contemplating writing to my solicitor when you put in an appearance just now. But I'll be hanged if I'm going to be bullied by the police!"

"Perhaps," said Ambrose, quietly, "you won't mind telling me how you heard of the affair last night – and why you didn't hear of it before. It's been in the newspapers."

"Do you imagine that when I come abroad for a holiday I bother myself with newspapers? I never read the damned French things – I'm not a linguist to begin with, and don't want to be. English is good enough for me. And I never saw an English newspaper till last night, when I picked one up here by chance – and then I read something about the murder. But only a brief mention of it – no details. I suppose they blared out the details on the previous days. All I know is that Hatton was found stabbed in those rooms at St. Oswald's College on the day when I was with him there – and at a time that seems to have fitted in with my visit. Naturally I felt perturbed, and when you appeared on the scene just now I imagined that the police had made one of their usual blunders and set me down as the murderer."

"And, of course, you can easily prove that you were not the murderer?"

Finmere opened his mouth to reply – stopped short – looked at Ambrose in silence for a few seconds – and then said:

"Damn it all, man! I've got no witnesses to prove it – if that's what you mean?"

"An alibi would do," retorted Ambrose.

"Or an alibi," said Finmere. "I left Hatton alive in those rooms and came out without seeing anyone – went straight to the station, as a matter of fact."

"Then, sir," replied Ambrose, "I'm sure you must see that your best course is to make a plain statement of what really happened. I have no power to compel you to make such a statement, though I ask you to do so – for your own interests – to say nothing of the help it may be in tracing the real criminal."

"Then you don't believe I killed the fellow?" Ambrose smiled.

"I've never said so, sir. And now, will you be good enough to give me an account of what took place when you saw Mr. Hatton in the room in which he was killed?"

Finmere thought for a moment.

"Very well, then," he said. "I would have preferred consulting my solicitor first, but if you can assure me that you're not going to take advantage of anything I say, I don't mind talking."

"Any advantage that I may take I don't think will be against you, Mr. Finmere. But you may help to put me on a right track. Before you begin I want to reiterate that I cannot compel you to make a statement – it must be purely voluntary on your part."

"I quite understand. Well, then, where would you like me to begin."

Ambrose had taken out his notebook. He replied:

"At the moment when you first entered the college, please. That was, I believe, about twelve or thirteen minutes after one o'clock."

"How do you know?"

"You were seen to go in, sir."

"I never saw anyone."

"Not in the porter's lodge?"

"No. I didn't meet a soul between the lodge and Mr. Henlow's rooms."

"I see. What were your reasons for visiting his rooms?"

Finmere explained what Ambrose already knew – the affair of the stained-glass window.

"You see," he went on, "from what Hatton had said when he visited the church I felt pretty sure that his wretched committee would reject my scheme, so I determined to make other arrangements. As soon as I made up my mind about it I realised there was no time to be lost if I wanted the design back before I came abroad. Hatton had told me about the meeting on the Tuesday, so I planned to break my journey to London at Exbridge and get the design."

"Did you expect to find the committee assembled?"

"I never thought about it – that is to say, the idea of their being out for luncheon did not occur to me. I knew the design would be in that room. That was all."

"And you found Hatton alone there?"

"I did. He was standing in the bow window when I went in."

"And then?"

"You will understand that I wasn't feeling very friendly towards him. I spoke to him, of course, and explained the object of my visit. His reply didn't put me in the best of tempers. He said the committee had, that morning, definitely turned down my scheme, and that it was no use applying to the chancellor for a faculty. 'There's the drawing,' he said.

'We stuck it on the bookcase so that we could all have a good look at it.'

"'Yes, and slang it, I suppose?' I replied.

"'Well,' he said, 'as a matter of fact we did say a few strong words about it. It really isn't suitable for a church window, you know.'

"That put my back up – and I confess I said a few strong words about him and his committee. While I was doing so I was trying to loosen the drawing pins, but they had been pressed in too tightly. Then I caught sight of a metal paper knife lying on the table and picked it up to force out the pins. I was in a bit of a temper, you see, and I suppose that made me careless. Anyhow, I tore the design a little with the point of the knife, which slipped as I was forcing out a pin."

"What was Hatton doing all this time?"

"He was standing with his back to the fire, silent for the most part."

"And then?"

"I spread the plan on the table and rolled it up. And now comes a thing which I can't quite explain. I've told you I was in a temper – I do lose my temper at times, I'm afraid, and you see when you've worked yourself up in a passion you don't always realise exactly what you're doing. Anyhow, to make a long story short, I must, though I didn't know it at the time, have kept that knife in my hand while I was rolling up the design. I mean I couldn't have laid it on the table again. I bid Hatton rather a curt good-day and went out of the room. It was only when I was half-way down the staircase, with the design in a roll tucked under my arm that I suddenly realised I was still grasping that knife in my right hand."

"Indeed? But this is very interesting. Please go on, Mr. Finmere. What did you do?"

"For a moment I hesitated. My first impulse was to go back. But I didn't want to see Hatton again – I was sick of him and his committee, I'm afraid. So I went on down the stairs, and when I got to the bottom I chucked the knife into the hole that was there. It fell among the loose earth at the bottom."

Ambrose whistled.

"The deuce it did, sir! That means that it can't have been the weapon that killed Mr. Hatton."

"I suppose," said Finmere, grimly, "that – to take another view of the question – it looks as if I had thrown the knife into that hole after I'd stabbed Hatton with it?"

"It fits in, certainly," replied the detective-sergeant, dryly, "but go on, please, sir. What happened as you left the college?"

"Nothing."

"You saw no one – in the college precincts?"

"No one."

"Nor anyone at the entrance gate?"

"No."

"Did you happen to notice the time when you left the college – I mean the exact time?"

"Yes, I did. I had a train to catch and I looked at my watch as I was walking through the quad. It was twenty-five minutes past one."

Ambrose made a rapid calculation. If this were so then the time-limit in which anyone could have come into the college unobserved and made for Henlow's rooms was narrowed down to a bare ten minutes – from one twenty-five to one thirty-five, one thirty-five being the time when the porter was back at his post.

"Tell me," he said, "when you got outside the college gate – into the street, you didn't see anyone about to come in?"

"No – not that I know of. I wasn't observing anyone particularly, of course."

"Try to remember, if you can, Mr. Finmere. Did you notice anyone outside the college?"

"Let me see – I turned to the right as I came out, to make my way to the station. There were several people near, on the pavement – yes – now I come to think of it I did glance at one fellow – he was coming across the street, from the other side, and he made a dash on to the pavement to avoid a motor car – I had to swerve slightly. I fancy he must have been short-sighted."

"Why?"

"Well – in the hasty glance I gave at him I remember he was wearing dark spectacles. And, yes – of course – he was a clergyman."

"A clergyman?"

"He had on a clerical hat – one of the old-fashioned round ones, with a flat top that you don't see so many of nowadays."

"Could you describe him further?"

"No, I couldn't. I didn't notice his face – or anything more about him – except the glasses and the hat."

Ambrose frowned – in thought. The fact that the individual in question was crossing the street just opposite the college might infer that he was making for the gateway. On the other hand, Finmere's scanty description of him was so very vague. Such a man was a familiar type in Exbridge. The university town abounded in clergy – dons, and retired parsons, incumbents of the many parishes, to say nothing of hosts of parsons who were constantly visiting the town. Exbridge was a regular rendezvous for members of the cloth. Dozens of them might be met in the streets at any time – many of them round-hatted and spectacled.

"Round-hatted and spectacled!" There seemed something familiar in the combination. Where was it he had heard the expression recently? Ah, he suddenly remembered. That rather garrulous Professor of Divinity, Dr. Blake, had told him that he always wore a round, clerical hat, and that, on a holiday, he had once appeared in dark spectacles and a Panama – and had, unwittingly, concealed his identity from a friend. But the parallel was not an exact one – the round hat and the spectacles had not gone together.

He looked up from his notes.

"And then – you took the train to London and called on Hastings – at St. John's Wood?"

"How the dickens do you know that?"

The detective-sergeant laughed.

"I've already interviewed Hastings, Mr. Finmere," he said, "and I may as well tell you that it was owing to that interview that I have had my doubts about your complicity in the case. I think you will admit that the fact of your being the last person seen to be with Hatton just before his death put you in a very questionable position – but when I found that you went straight to Hastings and told him all about your interview – even mentioning that you had made use of a weapon that we had every reason to believe was the fatal one – I couldn't, somehow, connect such an action with that of a guilty man. I'm very grateful to you for telling me all that took place, and I assure you that, in your own interests, you have done right in telling me. I shall write out your statement and get you to sign it. But there's something else I want you to do – also in your own interests, as well as in ours."

"What is that?"

"I want you to come back to England with me, Mr. Finmere – at once. Yes, sir" – as Finmere made a gesture of protest – "it is your wisest course. I want you to give evidence at the adjourned inquest, to begin with, but, in addition to this the fact of your hurrying home, directly you have found out your connection with the case, instead of remaining abroad will help to put you right in the eyes of those who question your innocence. Believe me, it is the best thing you can do."

Finmere, who had quite calmed down now, began to see the reasonableness of the detective-sergeant's suggestion. He had taken his pipe from his pocket and was slowly filling it."

"When do you want me to go?" he asked.

"Today, sir – if you will. There is a good train to Paris leaving here at twelve forty-five."

"That gives me very little time."

Ambrose shrugged his shoulders.

"It is important – really, Mr. Finmere."

Ambrose took a cigarette from his case and placed it in his lips. Then he felt in his pocket for matches. Finmere was lighting his pipe – he pushed a packet of matches across the table.

"Very well," he said, having made up his mind. "I will take your advice. I will see about packing in a few minutes."

"Good!"

Ambrose took up the packet of matches, one of those flat folders, containing paper matches. He raised the flap. There was a little stack of flat, red matches, with yellow heads, and on each match some wording.

> *DE LA FONTAINE.*
> *TABACS.*
> *CIGARETTES.*
> *DE LA FONTAINE.*
> *TABACS.*
> *CIGARETTES.*

Not for a moment did he let his face betray the extreme interest which the sight of these words aroused. For, in an instant, there flashed across his mind the half-burnt red match he had found in Henlow's rooms with the letters "TAINE" printed on the part that had not been consumed.

Had Finmere been telling only a plausible tale after all? Was his visit to Hastings, the artist, really a bit of bluff, artfully conceived to make out that although he had come straight from the scene of the murder he knew nothing about the crime.

Nonchalantly he tore off two matches, concealing one with the name "DE LA FONTAINE" and lighting his cigarette with the other. And said, carelessly enough:

"Handy matches, these, for one's waistcoat pocket. Do you always use them, Mr. Finmere?"

"No. But I bought some English tobacco here yesterday, and the man gave me that packet of matches."

"English tobacco?" echoed the detective-sergeant. "My pouch wants filling. May I ask where I can get some?"

"If you take the first turning on the right on the way from here to the station you'll find a little narrow street. There's a tobacconist and stationer's shop on the left side – only a few paces down. That's where I bought my tobacco."

"Thanks. Oh – by the way, sir – when you were with Mr. Hatton in that room did you smoke?"

"No; I didn't. Why do you ask?"

"I'm checking some cigarette stubs I found there," replied Ambrose, blandly.

"I never smoke the things," said Finmere. "Now, let me see – it's ten o'clock. You say that train leaves at a quarter to one. Shall I meet you at the station – or what?"

"I'll call back here, sir, a little before half-past twelve. Will that do?"

"Very well. We'll have a taxi to the station."

As Ambrose came out of the hotel grounds a man, who was lounging on a seat beside the lake, got up and came towards him.

"Pardon, monsieur," he said, raising his hat, "but Monsieur le Commissaire instructed me to ask you if you have made favourable progress with your affair?" and, turning back, for the moment, the lapel of his coat, he displayed a small metal badge.

"Give my compliments to Monsieur le Commissaire and tell him that Monsieur Finmere is travelling back with me to England today."

"He will be charmed, monsieur."

"We depart by the train at three-quarters after midday. Be sure to tell Monsieur le Commissaire that Monsieur Finmere accompanies me of his own free will – of course. But" – he hesitated – "I call for him at the Lion d'Or shortly before half-past twelve. I should like to make quite certain that he will be there."

"Rest assured, monsieur," replied the other, with a smile. "Monsieur Finmere will not leave without our knowing that he accompanies you."

"And give my best thanks to Monsieur le Commissaire."

"But certainly, monsieur!"

Ambrose found the tobacconist's shop in the little street, went in, and purchased a packet of tobacco.

"Et des allumettes," he added.

"Bien, monsieur," and the man behind the counter produced a flat booklet of matches. Ambrose filled his pipe – and used a match."

"Ah," he said, "your own matches, eh? I noticed the name 'de la Fontaine' over your shop door. Are they made specially for you?"

"Not exactly, monsieur. These matches are of a kind common in France. But it is possible to procure them plain and to have one's own name printed on them as an advertisement."

"A good idea," replied Ambrose. "And I suppose one cannot purchase them – with your name on, I mean – elsewhere?"

"You are right, Monsieur: that is impossible."

Ambrose saluted the man, and was about to leave the shop, when he remembered something. His landlady's little girl, a child of about eight years old, collected picture postcards. There was an array of these in the little shop. He chose one, and, knowing how much more the child would value it if it came by post, scribbled a line on it with his fountain pen and bought a stamp for it – every French tobacconist sells stamps. Outside, he posted it. He went back to his hotel, packed his small suitcase, ordered a light meal to be ready by a quarter to twelve, and, finally, made his way once more to the Lion d'Or. The man who had spoken to him was still sitting on a seat opposite the hotel entrance. He got up, waved his hand with a friendly gesture, and walked off.

At the doorway of the hotel a taxi was waiting, and in a minute or so Finmere appeared, ready for the journey. He was in a better temper than when Ambrose had first approached him.

"I little thought," he said, with a laugh, "when I started on my holiday that I should be escorted back by the police."

"But without handcuffs, sir!" retorted Ambrose, laughing in return. "I'm sorry to have interrupted your holiday though, Mr. Finmere. By the way, have you ever been to Evian-les-Bains before?"

"Many times," retorted Finmere. "The waters suit me better than those at any other spa. I was here only about three months ago. Whenever I feel a threat of my old complaint – rheumatic gout – I take it in time and nip it in the bud by taking the cure here."

"Oh!" replied Ambrose, and reflected in silence. Those matches could only be purchased at that particular tobacconist's at Evian-les-Bains!

XI

ON his return to Exbridge Ambrose reported the result of his visit to Evian-les-Bains to the superintendent.

"H'm," said the latter. "Looks as though Finmere has told a straight story, though it doesn't seem to help much. Anyhow, I'm glad you persuaded him to come back. And we'd better keep an eye on him for the present, now he's here."

"The snag about his story is that match," replied Ambrose. "By his own showing he very likely brought a packet back from Evian-les-Bains when he went there earlier in the year."

"Do you think there's much in it, really?"

"Well, sir – the name on the match – "

"I know. But it was only a few letters. Might not have belonged to 'de la Fontaine,' at all. There must be hundreds of varieties of these printed matches. And anyone of the members of that committee might have had a packet and used one of them at the meeting. Or, even if Finmere did use it, he may have lit his pipe while he was with Hatton."

"He says he didn't smoke there."

"Very likely. But he may not remember. He acknowledged he was in a devil of a temper at the time. Besides, there's another argument against it. Suppose he did strike a match. He'd hardly have dropped the burnt end in that bedroom wardrobe, would he? There was no occasion for him to go into that room at all."

"I'm not so sure of that," remarked Ambrose.

The superintendent shrugged his shoulders.

"I don't see it," he said. "I've thought all along that you've attached too much importance to that match."

"But you forget the broken shoelace, sir."

"What's that to do with it?"

"Perhaps it's a far-fetched notion. But there's a reason for everything. One shoe without a lace – and a bit of broken lace on the cupboard floor beside it. Why? The obvious answer is that someone found he had a broken lace in one of his shoes, and wanted another in a hurry. Where would he look for one? There was a bedroom handy – a bachelor's room – and he might very well count on finding an odd pair of shoes knocking about somewhere in it. He looks around and can see none. Then opens the wardrobe cupboard and strikes a match – it was rather dark at the bottom of the cupboard."

"Very pretty!" retorted Plestow, "but, as you admit yourself, a bit far-fetched. Do you mean to tell me that a murderer would have bothered about a bit of shoelace – with the body lying there all the time? Not much! If you follow up your theory you'll probably find that Henlow took the lace out of that shoe – before he went abroad. And as for that bit of a match – it might have been lying there for weeks – and probably was!"

"Anyhow I shall make inquiries – to find out whether any member of the committee used such matches."

"I suppose you must do that. Oh – by the way – since you left we've got in reports from all of them about that evening paper. Neither of them took one to the meeting!"

"That complicates matters still more, sir. I can't understand that newspaper at all."

The superintendent leaned back in his chair and reflected.

"I suppose it has occurred to you, Ambrose – in fact, I remember you mentioned it once – that there's one man who may have had that paper, and who had every opportunity of committing the murder."

"Who is that, sir?"

"The porter."

Ambrose nodded his head, slowly.

"You see," went on the superintendent, "we've only got his own word for his movements. If Finmere's story is correct and he left the college at twenty-five minutes past one, that porter would have a clear field till two o'clock – when the two workmen returned. All that he says about the people who came in and went out between one thirty-five and half-past two may be true enough, but it doesn't follow that he himself was at the gate every moment of the time –

and a very few minutes was all that was needed to get to Henlow's rooms and back and kill Hatton. Moreover the man had all the means of knowing exactly all the movements of the people concerned. He would see the members of the committee, with the exception of Hatton, leaving the college – and would know from experience they would not return till close on half-past two. He would know, also, that the two workmen would be absent for an hour from one to two.

"That's quite true, sir – but the motive? Why should he kill Hatton?"

"Why should anyone kill him?" answered the superintendent. "That's the weak point we've been up against all along. If we could only find a reason for getting Hatton out of the way we might get on a bit. But, for the life of me, I can't see one. Can you?"

"N-no," agreed Ambrose, slowly. "I can't, sir. Except that it looks as if, whatever reason there may have been, was a sudden one – I don't think anyone went into that room with a pre-conceived idea of killing Hatton."

"Very likely not. And I'm inclined to press that theory further. I'm inclined to think that whoever went into that room didn't expect to find anyone there."

"Yes, sir – but, on the other hand, doesn't it look as if Hatton was expecting someone? Else, why should he have arranged to have his luncheon there – and pretend he had letters to write?"

"He may have meant to write letters after all. We don't know. But, to get back to that porter. Assume that he thought

Hatton had gone out with the rest of them – they were all accustomed to go out, you know – he would jump to the conclusion that Henlow's rooms were empty, and the door unlocked. It was the one opportunity, bear in mind, that he had of getting into those rooms unobserved during Henlow's absence on the Continent. Williams had the only key, and kept the rooms locked."

"Why would he want to go into the rooms at all, sir?"

"Ah! There's a very plausible reason for that. When I interviewed Mr. Henlow he told me he had some rare books on those shelves of his. These college servants, porters, and so on, get to know things, Ambrose. I haven't spent ten years in a university city without finding that out! Rare books are not in my line, it's true, but I suppose there's a price to be got for them. And we have good reason, unfortunately, to know that someone's been at work here abstracting articles of value, and we suspect, don't we, there's more than one in the game. Very well, then, even if this porter isn't a principal, he may be one of the tools. Say he went into that room to get some of those books. Now we know from what Williams told us that Hatton had been standing in front of the bookcase. The design of that window which was pinned to it only covered a portion of the case – not that portion which contained Henlow's particular treasures – I saw that when Henlow checked them in my presence. We also know that Hatton was investigating the theft of Dr. Blake's miniature – probably connecting it with the other robberies which have taken place here. He may have had this in his mind when he was looking at Henlow's collection of books

– I don't mean that he was expecting that those books might be the next objective of the thief, but only that there was a mental connection.

"Now go a step further. Say that, after Finmere had left the room, Hatton went back into the recess formed by the oriel window. There's a curtain on either side of the recess, and anyone coming in at the door would not see him at first – especially if he was prepared to find the room empty. The porter comes in, and makes straight for the bookcase. Before he is aware of Hatton's presence he has begun taking out one or two of those books – and then, well, it's guesswork, of course, but Hatton might have tumbled to it, and charged the man with being a thief. A violent quarrel follows, in the course of which the porter stabs him to get rid of the incriminating evidence, and goes straight back to his post at the gate. What do you think of it, Ambrose?"

Ambrose had been listening attentively.

"It's plausible, sir – certainly. But there isn't enough to go upon, and, somehow – well – it doesn't seem to satisfy me."

"All the same," said the superintendent, "we can't afford to ignore it. I'm making inquiries about that porter's history and habits – and having an eye kept on him. But now, there's another matter. This letter came by the first post this morning. I knew, from your wire from Evian, that you would be here today, so I've taken no steps about it. You'd better follow it up – and see if there's anything in it."

He pushed the letter across the table. It was directed to the Superintendent of Police at Carnford, and signed by Miss Hatton, the murdered man's sister.

"DEAR SIR" – she wrote – "I should like very much to have a conversation with the police official who came to see me on the day on which my brother was killed. Perhaps you will kindly arrange this. Any morning this week would suit me if he could pay me a visit."

Ambrose glanced at his watch. It was past nine at night. He had left Paris that morning by the ten o'clock boat-train, after spending the night there with Finmere at an hotel.

"Very well, sir," he said. "I'll run out to Carnford tomorrow morning. I'll write her a line now to say I'm coming, and post it on my way to my rooms."

"No occasion for that," replied the superintendent, taking up the telephone receiver which stood on his table. "She's on the 'phone. I'll ring her up now . . . yes . . . thank you . . . hallo – hallo . . . yes.. Miss Hatton, please . . . yes . . . I'll hold on . . . Yes? Superintendent Plestow speaking, from the police station, Exbridge. In reply to your letter, Miss Hatton, my detective-sergeant will run out tomorrow morning. Will ten o'clock be too early for you to see him? . . . Good – thank you. Have you anything of importance to tell him? . . ."

He laid down the receiver.

"She says she has been looking through her brother's papers and there are one or two things which puzzle her. Dare say it's a fuss about nothing. But you'd better go. . . Goodnight, Ambrose."

"Goodnight, sir."

The detective-sergeant picked up his small suitcase, for he had come there, with Finmere, straight from the station, and Finmere, after a brief interview with the superintendent, had gone to an hotel in Exbridge for the night. He made his way to his lodgings.

"Glad to see you safe back, sir," said his landlady. "I've got a nice little hot supper for you. I had your wire saying you would be home some time tonight. Your postcard to Muriel came this morning, and she's ever so pleased with it, Mr. Ambrose. I think it was so kind of you to remember her. She's asleep now, of course, but she wants to see you about that postcard – she can't understand the words that are printed on it, and I'm sure I can't, either. Some foreign language, ain't they, Mr. Ambrose?"

Ambrose laughed.

"Well, it's a French card, you see, Mrs. Glover, and they have a way of speaking and writing in French over there. I'll translate it for her."

"I was sure you would, Mr. Ambrose – there now, while I'm talking you're wanting for your supper – I'll go and dish it up."

There was no time, however, to see Muriel the next morning before he left his lodgings. He wanted an hour or so at the police station before he ran out to see Miss Hatton. Finally he drew up in his car at her house at Carnford a little after ten, and was shown into the room in which Miss Hatton had received him on the occasion of his former visit.

She looked worn and tired, and her face bore traces of the strain and mental suffering through which she had gone. But her quiet dignity had not forsaken her.

"It is kind of you to come," she said, "especially as you may think that I am wasting your time. But I was anxious to see you. It is a very painful subject – but may I ask if you have any hopes of solving the problem of my poor brother's murder?"

"I have been doing nothing else but trying to solve it – since I saw you here, Miss Hatton."

"And – ?" Her eyebrows rose questioningly.

"At present," he replied, "it is difficult to estimate what progress I may have made. The case is by no means a simple one. But you may rest assured that we are doing our best. One of the chief stumbling blocks in the way is the question of motive. If only we could get a hint as to why anyone should have killed your brother!"

"I know. I have been thinking of that, also. I cannot imagine anyone wanting to do such a dreadful thing. And since you were here I have been going through my brother's papers to see if there was any indication of his being in trouble – or having an enemy."

"And have you discovered anything, Miss Hatton?"

"I don't know," she replied, slowly. "That is why I wanted to consult you. My brother was reticent – even with me – in his private affairs. He was also extremely methodical. His papers were in perfect order in the drawers of his desk here – letters, specifications and drawings relating to his work in connection with ecclesiastical architecture, and so on. There is nothing there to arouse any suspicion. But, I think I told you, he had a curious hobby. He was interested in crime, Mr. Ambrose – especially in the detection of crime. I mentioned, didn't I, how he loved to read detective stories up to a certain point, and then try to work out the solution himself?"

"Yes – you told me that."

"I also mentioned that for three or four evenings previous to his death he was deeply immersed in one of these problems and that he suddenly said: 'I've got it at last.' You asked, at the time, if he referred to a book afterwards to verify his theory, and I told you he didn't."

The detective-sergeant leaned forward with interest.

"I remember perfectly," he said.

She went on:

"My brother was in the habit of jotting down these problems of his in a notebook, making very brief and abbreviated entries. I've frequently been with him in the evening after dinner when he was using this book, but I suppose he knew I was not much interested in his hobby, and he never showed it to me. Now I've been looking at this book, Mr. Ambrose. For the most part it's quite unintelligible to me. But – on the last two pages" – she broke off suddenly – "there's someone named 'Cosway,' Mr. Ambrose, and I'm wondering who he is."

Ambrose almost jumped in his seat.

"'Cosway!'" he cried. "I can tell you who Cosway is, and I think I know something about that last problem Mr. Hatton was working at. Cosway is the name of a famous miniature artist and one of his miniatures was recently stolen from the collection of Dr. Blake. And Dr. Blake has told me that your brother was trying to find out who was the thief – and had said he thought he had succeeded in doing so. Why do you ask?"

"Because the name occurs in these curious notes made by my brother. I had never heard him mention it, you see."

"May I look at the notes?"

"Certainly. That is why I asked you to come here. You made me see, on thinking it over, that it was important for you to know my poor brother's habits – even his hobbies."

She opened a drawer in her brother's desk and took out several packets of papers, and some notebooks.

"You can, if you wish it, take all these with you and go through them, but I don't think you will find anything to help you. For the most part they are what I told you just now – notes on architectural subjects, some bundles of receipted accounts, and some private correspondence. I have examined them all carefully. But there is this particular notebook – headed 'Detection problems' – let me see – yes!"

She produced a small, leather-bound notebook, and held it out to him.

"Here it is."

Ambrose opened the book she gave him, and rapidly glanced through it. Hatton had been methodical, each page being devoted to a "problem," and headed with a title. Some of these titles he recognised as those of detective stories he had read. The symbol of X was used to denote the unknown criminal. Rough jottings, speculations, and so forth, followed, and, generally, there was the conclusion – stated in the form of an algebraical solution:

"X = the butler"; "X = the stranger in the train," and so on.

The last page, however, contained no such conclusion, though the symbol of X was freely used. It was as follows:

"Cosway.

PURCHASE.	FTONBRST	MVOESGTH
HEMLTACB	VSTROUZI	CTYBSBHG
LONJKRTS	SBRFJYXI	

August 4th:

X possesses HEMLTACB vide his diary.

X in Blake's rooms. Cosway disappears.

Provost of Malvern's Corot. Equally accessible to X. Impossible!

Yet: (I) X and the B.'s.

        (II) X and Stock Exchange.

Query – If so, where kept till disposal? Any indication from X?

August 10th:

X indicates a possible one.

Tubby's whisky? Ask him.

August 26th:

Tubby told me. Try it."

Ambrose studied this strange document with knitted brows.

"If he'd only said who X was!" he murmured.

"Can you make anything of it?"

"I may do. I think it's very important, Miss Hatton. You see, your brother not only mentions the Cosway miniature, but the Corot that was stolen from the Provost of Malvern. It is evident he was on the track of the thief – besides, he told Dr. Blake he was. Let me see – there are three dates indicated. I wish we could find out where your brother went on them. On August the fourth he seems to have seen X's diary. On the tenth he seems, again, to have been with X. And on the twenty-sixth he saw an individual named 'Tubby' – apparently to ask him something about his whisky. Now, what could that mean?"

"I think I may be able to help you," replied Miss Hatton, "if you will wait for a few moments."

She left the room, and returned presently with a small book in her hand.

"This is my diary," she explained, "and sometimes I entered my brother's movements as well as my own. Let me see – August the fourth. Of course, that was the first Tuesday in the month. Here it is – Francis at his 'Diocesan Committee.' Now, what is the next date? The tenth – Thursday – no, I haven't entered anything about him – but I can tell you where he went in that day, all the same. I see that I spent that day at Derringford, with friends I have there, and I remember that my brother motored me in to Exbridge, where I took the train, and met me at the station about five o'clock. He told me he hadn't been home – he had lunched at Dr. Blake's and attended a county meeting of some sort in the afternoon. The last date – the twenty-sixth – yes, I've made an entry that he went to London that day."

"Evidently to see 'Tubby,'" rejoined Ambrose. "Now, Miss Hatton, do you know by any chance, who is meant by 'Tubby'?"

"I can't be certain, but it must have been someone with whom my brother was familiar. There is a man he knows very well, who answers to the description – a short, stout man."

"Yes?"

"Sir Wilfred Haynes – a barrister, I think. I know he has rooms in the Middle Temple. He was up at Exbridge with my brother in his undergraduate days. He stayed with us some time ago, and I have a faint recollection of Francis calling him 'Fatty' – or it may have been 'Tubby.' I don't know."

"Oh, but this is excellent, Miss Hatton. Now, I want you to try to remember, if you can. This fourth of August. You see it was the meeting of the Consultative Committee – and it's very significant. Whose diary could he have seen? And when? Can you recollect anything he may have said when he returned that might throw a light on things?"

"I'm afraid I can't. Let me think – the Consultative Committee – yes – he was home about six o'clock. Yes –

wait a minute – there was something he told me – ah – I remember. He said he had lunched at a rather nice new restaurant in George Street – Mr. Stanhope had persuaded him to go with him there."

Stanhope! The little artist with the beard. One of the two men who had found Hatton dead in that armchair. The other was Kershaw. They had come into the college together – the first of the committee to return from luncheon.

A sudden thought rose to the mind of the detective-sergeant. Had these two returned together? Was it possible that Stanhope had returned much earlier – just after Finmere's departure – and remained within the college precincts till Kershaw came in at the gate – only joining him then. He must find out from Kershaw.

Was Stanhope this mysterious X? The two men had lunched together on August the fourth. Could it have been then that Hatton had seen the diary, which seemed to have had that apparently nonsensical string of letters written in it?

Miss Hatton broke into his reverie.

"What can be the meaning of those curious sets of letters?" she asked. "Is it a cryptogram?"

"Not exactly. But I think I know what they allude to. I'm infinitely obliged to you for this information, Miss Hatton."

"Do you think it will help you to trace the murderer, Mr. Ambrose?"

"That depends upon whether it is directly connected with your brother's death – and I have strong suspicions that it is. I look on it something like this: Mr. Hatton, interested as he was in any problem connected with crime, had set himself the task of trying to find out who had stolen Dr. Blake's miniature. In some way or other that we don't know yet he connected the robbery with an individual whom he seems to have come across on August the fourth, the day when the Consultative Committee met. Now, it is a significant fact that at the next meeting of the committee he had planned to remain in Mr. Henlow's rooms during the luncheon hour; significant, because, still bent on solving his problem, that was the day when we might expect him to have the opportunity of meeting X again. And I am inclined to believe, Miss Hatton, that he had arranged to meet X. in Mr. Henlow's rooms while the rest of the committee were lunching."

"And have you any suspicion as to the identity of X?"

The detective-sergeant thought rapidly. Beside the possibility of Stanhope there occurred to his mind Williams, the scout – his alibi would have to be investigated again – and the superintendent's theory about the porter. Then, suddenly, he remembered Finmere's story of the clergyman who had been crossing the street, towards the entrance of the college, as Finmere came out of it. He glanced at Hatton's notes again. That word "impossible!" It might easily apply to such an individual. It would seem impossible that a clergyman – probably some well-known Exbridge don or resident – should be mixed up in a series of robberies.

He replied to Miss Hatton's direct question.

"I can't hazard any opinion yet," he said. "You have given me much to think about, though, and I shall try to follow up certain suggestions which these notes seem to imply. One of them will be to see Sir William Haynes as soon as possible."

"I'm afraid I don't know his exact address."

"That doesn't matter, Miss Hatton. I shall soon find out, from a London directory. And now, please, you must let me take this notebook of your brother's with me, and I must ask you not to mention a word about it or about our conversation – to anyone – not to Mr. Hatton's most intimate friends, should you come across any. This is important."

"You may rely on me," she answered. "I shall keep my own counsel. You will let me know what happens?"

"I hope we may be able – in due time – to acquaint a jury with the result of our investigations," he replied.

The first thing Ambrose did on his return to Exbridge was to call on Dr. Blake, the Divinity Professor, and ask to see him. He was told that the professor was at that moment lecturing to a vacation School of Clergy, but that he was sure to return to his room within about a quarter of an hour. He showed the man his card, and asked to be allowed to wait. After a moment's hesitation the man showed him into the professor's study.

"I have orders, sir," he explained, "not to admit strangers, but in your case I suppose –" He broke off.

"I'm not going to run away with anything – and the professor knows me."

"Yes, sir. I remember you came to see him the other day. That is why I have allowed you to come in."

"One up to you, my friend!" murmured Ambrose, as the servant left the room. Then the smile which had broken out on his face broadened. He sat down at the professor's table, helped himself to a sheet of paper out of the paper rack, took Hatton's notebook from his pocket, and slowly copied out, in black letters, the eight combinations of letters. Then he blotted the paper, and put it, folded, in his waistcoat pocket.

The professor came in with an array of books tucked under his arm.

"Good morning, young man," he began. "I hope you haven't been trying to open my treasure chest – though I've got a key padlock on it now."

"So I see, sir. No, I haven't come with any nefarious intentions."

The professor put down his books and looked keenly at the younger man.

"Still trying to find out who murdered poor Hatton?" he asked.

"I am, sir."

"Umph! Made any progress?"

"I hope so. But it takes time, sir. I've come about the case now. I want your help again."

"Again? Have I been any help, then?"

"I think so, sir. What you told me last time I saw you has certainly been of use to me. I won't keep you long. I want you to show me that letter lock which was on your Corean chest when your miniature was stolen, if you will, please!"

"The original lock. Oh, yes. I've got it here."

He unlocked a drawer in his desk and produced it.

"Now, sir – will you kindly set the combination for opening it?"

As the professor did so, Ambrose took the folded paper from his waistcoat pocket. The professor pushed the lock across the table towards him.

"There," he said. "I've set it."

But Ambrose did not take it up immediately.

"Besides the key word," he said, "there should be seven other combinations of letters round the lock. I think you will find the word and all the combinations on this slip of paper."

Dr. Blake unfolded the slip, and read it.

"PURCHASE. Yes, that's the key word – and these others – Now, look here, young man," he exclaimed, laying down the paper. "Are you a policeman or a professional conjurer? That's what I want to know. You couldn't have guessed these combinations. How did you do it?"

"Simply enough," said Ambrose, laughing. "You told me Mr. Hatton had examined that letter lock. Well, he'd evidently written down all the combinations on a notebook. That's where I found them – and copied them. But the point is a serious one, Dr. Blake. He seems to have found out that someone else had got hold of one of those combinations, and, if he had, as I showed you the other day, it would have given him the clue to the key word. Now, would you mind taking that new padlock off your safe, and replacing it with this letter lock – Good! Thank you, sir. Now, please, set the combination to open the lock as you would have done if anyone were standing by – concealing the key word – yes, that's it. Do you see, sir? I can easily read the combination – HEMLTACB. That's what happened, you may depend upon it!"

"Yes, but," said the professor, "who was it who got hold of that combination, I should like to know."

"So should I. Now, in his notes, Hatton gives a hint that it was someone who had access to your rooms. Of course that's obvious. But can you remember in whose presence you have opened that safe."

The professor wheeled round, irritably.

"My dear young man," he said. "I could give you a list of half the dons of the university to whom I've shown my miniatures – to say nothing of dozens of other friends!"

"Let me suggest a few persons, sir. Did you ever show them to the porter at St. Oswald's College – or to a servant named Williams there?"

"They are neither dons nor my personal friends," rejoined Dr. Blake, caustically. "No. Certainly not!"

"Or to a Mr. Stanhope – an artist?"

"Stanhope? Why, yes. I know him quite well. I have shown them to him, I believe."

"Ah!"

"Now, don't tell me you suspect Stanhope!" retorted the professor. "That's impossible, you know."

"Not impossible, sir."

"Well. Not at all likely. Of course not."

"One more question, sir. Did you ever set the combination in the presence of a clergyman who wears dark glasses?"

"Oh, come now, young man! Don't be absurd. Half the clergy here wear glasses of some sort. I couldn't pick you out any particular one among 'em! But may I ask what all this has to do with the tracing of Hatton's murderer – if anything?"

"I can't answer that question, yet, sir. I wish I could. But I've got a notion that I'm going to follow up. I fancy that Hatton was on the track of the man who stole your Cosway – and other things as well – and that he had made an appointment concerned with his discovery in the room in which that committee met. And if this is correct there must be some connection with the murder. Hatton was killed in that room, you know."

The professor had seated himself in his chair, leaning back in an attitude of thought.

"Yes – I see what you mean," he replied, slowly. "It's intricate, but it's feasible. I also gather that you have further, and more definite suspicions. But I can't bring myself to imagine that Mr. Stanhope – "

"You won't mention his name to anyone – in this connection, please, sir?"

"I shall respect your confidence, young man, but, if I were given to racing slang, I should say you were backing the wrong horse."

"I'm not backing any horse, sir," replied Ambrose, as he got up to go. "I never bet on uncertainties in my profession, and, to follow up your metaphor, I have no favourite in the field. I want to make sure of the winner before I act."

"You'll find him a dark horse," said the professor, dryly.

"So I think, sir. Good morning – and thank you very much."

XII

THE first thing Ambrose did on leaving Dr. Blake was to look up Sir Wilfred Haynes' address in the London Directory. Having found it, and ascertained that the barrister was on the telephone, he put through a trunk call, with a view to making an appointment. Here, however, he was disappointed, for he was answered, apparently by a clerk, to the effect that Sir Wilfred was absent from his chambers, being retained on a case at the Downshire Assizes. The clerk went on to say that if the matter was urgent he could communicate with Sir Wilfred, who was expected to return the next day or the following – when the case on which he was engaged was concluded.

Ambrose had to content himself with the clerk's promise to ring him up as soon as he could fix an interview with Sir Wilfred.

Having settled this matter as far as he could he was summoned from his room at the police station to attend a conference with Colonel Langdale, who had just come in.

He found the chief constable closeted with the superintendent, who was telling him the result of Ambrose's visit to Evian-les-Bains. A long conversation followed, in the course of which Ambrose produced Hatton's notebook, and recounted the progress he had made that morning. Colonel Langdale listened attentively.

"Well," he said, presently, "if anything comes of it, and it transpires that the two crimes are connected, we shall pull off a big thing. Let me see, now. You seem to have succeeded in bringing four men under suspicion – the porter, Williams, the college servant, Stanhope, and an unknown person."

"I think we can rule out Williams, sir," said the superintendent, consulting one of the numerous papers relating to the case which lay on his desk. "His alibi is a pretty sound one, especially as we know for certain, both from what Wilkins told us he saw from across the street, and from Mr. Finmere's own corroboration of it, that Hatton was certainly alive after Williams had left him."

"Very well, then," said the chief constable, "let's eliminate Williams. Now, how about the porter?"

"Well, sir," replied the superintendent. "I was telling the sergeant here only last evening that the porter had every opportunity of committing the crime – and telling half-truths afterwards to shield himself from suspicion. But, on thinking it over, I don't feel satisfied. Since then I've managed to get a little information about him – he's well-known in Carnford, and bears an exemplary character. That, of course, may mean nothing when it comes to murder. I'm keeping him under observation, though, sir."

"Good! Well, suppose, for the time being, we give him the benefit of the doubt. Now let's take this little artist chap – Stanhope. What about him?"

"He told me, jokingly, that he had an alibi," said Ambrose.

"Did you accuse him, then?"

"No, sir. Certainly not. I was only telling him, in the course of conversation, that, unless they could prove the contrary, all the members of that committee, himself included, naturally incurred suspicion. That's what made him say he had an alibi."

"And has he?"

"We've got to go into that, sir, now that he's come under suspicion. He said he returned to the college with Mr. Kershaw. We must ask Mr. Kershaw if he did."

The chief constable nodded.

"And," he went on, "this other fellow – the parson whom Finmere saw crossing the street. Rather vague, isn't it?"

"We can't afford to throw it over because it's vague," replied Ambrose.

"Quite so," said the superintendent, "but it's rather like looking for a needle in a haystack, all the same."

"I've got a notion about it, sir," rejoined Ambrose, "that I'll follow up. But we have to account for two other items."

"What are they?" asked Colonel Langdale.

"That evening paper – and the half-burnt match."

"Stanhope might have brought that paper with him," reflected the chief constable, "and as to the match – what's your opinion of that, superintendent?"

"I told Ambrose last evening. I don't think very much of it. Of course, Finmere may have brought back some of those matches from his previous visit to Evian – and used one when he went to get his drawing, but, as I said last night, it's hardly likely he'd have thrown it in the wardrobe – though Ambrose has rather a far-fetched theory about that." And he proceeded to explain it.

"Umph!" exclaimed the chief constable, glancing at his watch. "Well, what do you propose to do now, sergeant?"

"I shall get into communication with Mr. Kershaw, sir – and interview Sir Wilfred Haynes as soon as possible. And I want to have a chat with that porter."

"Very well. Let me see – the adjourned inquest is on Thursday, isn't it? Good! I hope you'll get hold of something definite before then. I must be off now. I want to have a word or two with Mr. Henlow, if I can get hold of him. I haven't seen him since he came back from Switzerland."

Colonel Langdale came out of the police station and made his way, with the somewhat jaunty military bearing which was characteristic of him, up the High Street. At the entrance to St. Oswald's College he accosted the porter.

"Is Mr. Henlow in his rooms?"

"I think you'll find him there, sir. If not, he's probably in the college. I haven't seen him go out this morning."

The chief constable passed on, entered the inner quad, and slowly ascended the staircase in the corner. Here was the scene of the crime. Would his men solve it? He tapped at the door of Henlow's room.

"Come in."

Henlow was seated at his table, writing: a pile of books and manuscripts before him.

"Hallo, Henlow!" said Colonel Langdale, who knew him well. "Disturbing you, I'm afraid."

"Not at all, colonel. Glad to see you."

"Well," said the chief constable, as he took a proffered chair and produced his cigarette case. "A pretty kettle of fish you've provided for us unfortunate policemen, eh? What do you mean by it?"

"I didn't provide it! Though some of the newspaper reporters seem to think I did. I've been pestered with them."

"You would be! You have my sympathy, Henlow. It was a nasty affair to happen in your rooms."

"It seems to have come of poor Hatton turning my room into a restaurant," replied Henlow, grimly. "He'd never done such a thing before – or any of the others, either."

"Gave you a shock when you heard of it, didn't it?"

"Indeed it did. I was on my way back from Geneva, and happened to buy an English paper while the train was waiting at Vallorbes – at the customs examination. That's the first intimation I had of it. I can't understand it. Your superintendent was on the spot pretty quickly, I hear, wasn't he?"

"Didn't waste much time. Hatton couldn't have been dead an hour when we began our investigations."

"And yet – you haven't traced the murderer?"

The chief constable shook his head.

"Not yet. It's a complicated case, Henlow."

"I don't know anything about your police methods, Langdale, but I should have thought that knife of mine would have been something to go upon – fingerprints, you know."

"Not much use, I'm afraid. You see – well – it looks very much now as if that knife didn't come into the case at all. I don't think it's going to help us.

"But surely – how else could he have been killed?"

"Plenty of other weapons about."

"But it looked so obvious."

"You can't always count on the obvious."

"What makes you think Hatton wasn't killed with that knife?"

"Ah! I mustn't tell you that, yet, Henlow. But we have a very good reason. It'll probably come out at the adjourned inquest. I suppose you'll attend it?"

"Out of curiosity and interest, yes – I may. But I haven't any evidence to give."

"N-no. I suppose not. My superintendent has seen you, so he tells me."

"Yes. But I fear I wasn't of any use to him."

"I'd like to ask you a question or two, Henlow. I'm not doing the spade work, but I'm responsible, you know. Now, between ourselves – you must have been turning things over in your mind – you know all the members of this committee. Is there anyone of them – "

"I can't conceive of one," broke in Henlow. "I've thought, of course – but it looks impossible."

"Stanhope – for example? I'm speaking in confidence, Henlow."

"Stanhope!" echoed the other, with a short laugh. "Ridiculous! He's a fiery little fellow, I admit, but it's only his bark. Stanhope wouldn't injure a fly! What makes you ask me such a question?"

The chief constable only shrugged his shoulders in reply.

"I have known Hatton and Stanhope for some years," went on Henlow, "and have had plenty of opportunity for observing them together when they came to the committee here. Except that they disagreed pretty sharply at times on questions relating to art and architecture, they were very friendly towards each other. I think you are on the wrong track, colonel."

"I didn't say I was on any particular track," replied the colonel, evasively. "I have to take everything into consideration – and even the best of friendships may sometimes be broken down by a quarrel."

"I can't imagine Stanhope having any cause for starting a quarrel with Hatton."

"Or Hatton starting it?" suggested the chief constable.

Henlow looked at him curiously.

"I don't quite follow," he said.

Colonel Langdale took a fresh cigarette from his case, and lit it.

"I don't mind telling you, Henlow," he said, "that we have reason for believing that poor Francis Hatton was deliberately asking for trouble. Don't ask me to explain further. Whether he was asking Stanhope – or anyone else, is the problem we have to solve. And it is not an easy one."

Henlow was silent for a moment or two. Then he asked:

"Are you calling in the help of Scotland Yard, Langdale?"

"I haven't – as yet," replied the colonel. "I know folks think we ought to do so whenever we country police are face to face with a big thing. But Scotland Yard – though I wouldn't say so officially – isn't always infallible, and I happen to have a particularly smart man investigating. I don't see why he shouldn't have his chance."

"Your superintendent? Yes, he appeared to me to be a shrewd individual."

"No. Not Plestow. He's a first-rate man, too. I mean one of our detective-sergeants – Ambrose. He hasn't been to see you, I think."

"No. I don't know him."

"Ah! Stout fellow, Ambrose! Well, I must be going. You'll treat this little chat as confidential, Henlow? Especially anything I may have said about Stanhope."

"Of course. But there I think you're wrong, Langdale. Goodbye – I hope you'll catch the fellow, whoever he is."

The chief constable made his way out of the college. In the High Street he met Ambrose, and stopped to speak to him for a moment.

"I'm on my way to see that porter," explained Ambrose. "I've a few questions I want to ask him."

"Ah!" said Colonel Langdale. "I've just been having a chat with Mr. Henlow, but I don't think there's much information to be got from that quarter."

"No, sir. The superintendent told me about his interview with him, and I haven't thought it worthwhile to see him."

"Quite so," replied the colonel, nodding as he passed on."

Ambrose found the porter in his lodge, and came to the point at once.

"I want to ask you something," he said. "Just carry your mind back to the day of the murder. You were here at one thirty-five."

"That's right, sergeant. When I came back from the post office."

"Very well. Now I've ascertained that a certain person may have come in here shortly before that – "

"I shouldn't have seen him – "

"I know that. But I want to find out if you can tell me anything about him."

"Who was he, sergeant?"

"Ah! That's just the point. I've only got a very meagre description of him. I'll tell you. A clergyman, wearing one of those rather old-fashioned, round, flat-topped clerical hats, and dark glasses. Now, do you know anyone who tallies with that description?"

The porter smiled.

"Several, sergeant! But, as it happens, I might give a guess as to this particular parson. I know one of 'em that wears that sort of hat and dark specs – he comes in here from time to time. He's a friend of Mr. Henlow's – and of the Bursar, too."

"Who is he?"

"The Reverend Gilbert. He's a private coach, sergeant. Lives in rooms somewhere in St. Edmund's Street. He helps sometimes on Sundays at the services at St. Wilfrid's. Oh, yes – he might very likely have come in."

"And you say he's a friend of Mr. Henlow's?"

"That's so, sergeant."

"So that he'd know his way to Mr. Henlow's rooms?"

The porter laughed.

"Of course he would. As I say, I often see him coming in or going out."

"You didn't see him going out on that Tuesday?"

"No"

"Yet you might have done – without knowing it!"

"How the deuce do you make that out?"

"Have you ever read G. K. Chesterton's *Father Brown* stories?"

"No. What's that got to do with it?"

"You read the one about 'the Invisible Man,' and you'll see," replied Ambrose. "Where did you say this Mr. Gilbert lives?"

"In St. Edmund's Street – but I'm not sure of the number."

"All right. I'll soon find out. But I think now I'll see Mr. Henlow first."

"You won't find him in, sergeant; he went out just before you came – after your boss had been to see him."

"The Bursar, then."

"He's away for the week."

"It doesn't matter. St. Edmund's Street, you say. Good-morning."

Ambrose soon found Mr. Gilbert's lodgings, and inquired for him of his landlady.

"Mr. Gilbert is away, sir."

"Oh. You don't happen to know where?"

"He's with a reading party – in the Isle of Wight. He generally makes up a reading party in the long vacation."

"I see. When did he go?"

"About a month ago, sir."

"Oh! Then he wasn't here on the eighth of this month – the first Tuesday?"

"Oh, yes, sir. He was here then."

"But you told me a moment ago he's been away for a month."

"So he has, sir, in a manner of speaking. But you see, he comes back on weekends to take Sunday duty at St. Wilfrid's Church, and on this particular weekend, instead of returning to the Isle of Wight on the Monday morning as he usually does, he waited till Tuesday afternoon. He had to take a wedding at St. Wilfrid's on Tuesday morning – the vicar's away."

"Had to take a wedding? What time was it?"

"Twelve o'clock, I think, sir."

Ambrose thought for a moment.

"He came back here to lunch afterwards, I suppose?"

"No, sir – he didn't. He had lunch out. He came back just before three – to get his bag to take to the station."

"You can give me his address?"

He wrote it down in his notebook – an address at Freshwater, and thanked the woman for her information. As he walked away he was wondering if he ought to communicate with this Mr. Gilbert at once, or await his return for the next Sunday's duty at St. Wilfrid's. If the former, it meant either telephoning to the police in the Isle of Wight asking them to make inquiries, or going there himself to do so. The public read the details of a great trial, with the police evidence, but rarely appreciate the long, patient, and tedious process of inquiries which often precedes the evidence of a brief half-hour. The investigator of a crime, particularly if that crime be murder, cannot afford to ignore any detail, however trivial it may appear to be on the surface, which, in any way may bear on the main question.

Mr. Gilbert would have to be seen. That was certain. There might be nothing in it, of course, but the brief inquiries Ambrose had already made had produced sufficient data to be followed up. As he walked back to the police station he tabulated these data mentally. As thus:

1. Finmere declared he had seen a clergyman wearing a round hat and dark glasses crossing the street towards the entrance of the college just

before it was pretty certain the crime had been committed.

2. The porter had recognised the description as applying to Mr. Gilbert, and had said that Gilbert was in the habit of visiting the college and making his way to Henlow's rooms.

3. The mysterious "X" was evidently someone known in university circles. Hatton's notes showed he had access to Dr. Blake.

4. Gilbert was in Exbridge at the time, and did not return to his rooms in the luncheon hour – but went back to them shortly before three o'clock.

5. On the *Father Brown* theory – quite a plausible one – he might have left the college before half-past two, without the porter noticing him. It fitted in with the time exactly!

On the whole he came to the conclusion that he would prefer to see Gilbert himself. It was too late, however, to run down to the Isle of Wight that day. But he had another task before him He must see Kershaw.

Kershaw he found, on consulting the telephone directory at the police station, was not on the 'phone. He was Vicar of Hartlebury, a small village about twenty-five miles from Exbridge. So Ambrose determined to run there in the police car and take his chance of finding his quarry at home.

As a matter of fact the Rev. James Kershaw, registered, it will be remembered, in George Wilkins' inquisitive mind as "the waiter out for a spree," was at home – white tie and all – and received the detective-sergeant in his study. The latter explained that he was investigating the Hatton case, and wanted to make some further inquiries.

"But I've told the police people all I know," said Kershaw, "and repeated it at the opening of the inquest."

"Yes, sir," replied Ambrose, "but there are one or two points on which we are not quite clear – and I thought you might help me."

"Go on," said Kershaw. "What are they?"

Ambrose proceeded very carefully. He was anxious to arouse no suspicions concerning Stanhope in the other's mind. So he began with a question or two about the finding of the knife, and followed them up with some inquiries as to the exact position of the body in the chair. Then he looked at his notebook.

"Let me see," he said. "You had been lunching with Mr. Stanhope, hadn't you, sir?"

"No, no," replied Kershaw. "I hadn't been lunching with him."

"I see – oh, yes – of course – you and he were the first of your committee to return to the college. You walked back with him along the High Street."

"I can't see that it matters," answered Kershaw, "but I never said that – exactly. We went into the college together, to be quite precise. As a matter of fact he had returned just before I did. He was standing at the entrance to the college – smoking his pipe – when I came up. Then we both began talking, and went in."

"Oh, it's all the same, of course," said the detective-sergeant, casually. "I only wanted to make quite sure that none of the others came in before you two. Thank you, sir. That's all, I think."

Kershaw looked at him.

"You don't suspect either of the others, I trust?" he asked.

"Certainly not, sir. Not for a moment. But we like to have everything in exact order."

Kershaw offered him tea – which he accepted. The two men talked on general topics, avoiding the murder. Kershaw got on to his hobby – mediaeval decorations of churches, and found Ambrose not only interested, but possessed of a keen appreciation of art. And Kershaw persuaded him to have a look at his church – showing him a beautiful old chancel screen he had recently restored.

But Ambrose, all the time, was really interested in something else. Could Stanhope produce that alibi to which he had jokingly alluded when he had met him in the London restaurant?

That remained to be seen!

Yes – Gilbert or Stanhope? Which was the more likely trail?

At all events both must be followed up. More work, and more patience.

XIII

AMBROSE, beginning to plan his day's work on the following morning, suddenly found his first task provided for. The telephone bell rang, and on answering it he received a message from Sir Wilfred Haynes himself.

Sir Wilfred said that he had returned from the Downshire Assizes the previous night and that his clerk had, that morning, told him that the Exbridge police wished to communicate with him. He would be in his chambers until two o'clock. Ambrose replied that he would take the next train to London and call on him.

On consulting the time-table he found he had half an hour to spare before he need start for the station. He spent the half-hour in consultation with the superintendent. The latter agreed with him that it was important to test Stanhope's alleged alibi as speedily as possible.

"I'll see to that," he said. "Stanhope lives at Derringford, doesn't he. Yes . . . all right . . .he's on the 'phone. I'll ring him up presently and find out if he can see me if I motor over. If he's got an alibi we shall have to prove it – probably here. With good luck I ought to do that today, and we shall know one way or the other. You get off to London, and find out, what Hatton meant about 'Tubby's whisky!'"

Ambrose started for the station. He was, of course, in mufti, and there was nothing to suggest the policeman in the well-dressed young man who took a return ticket to London.

The train was already in the station as he came on to the platform. Selecting a smoking compartment, in which two or three men were seated, he got in and unfolded the morning paper he had just bought at the bookstall and began reading it.

Someone got in at the last moment – just as the train started – and took a seat on the opposite side of the compartment. Ambrose did not notice him at first – he was reading his paper intently. After a while he laid down his paper, took out his pipe, began to fill it, and glanced round casually at his travelling companions.

The man who had last entered was reading the *Church Times*, holding it spread out before his face. It needed little deduction to assume that he was probably a cleric, and the assumption proved correct as he lowered the paper a little, and Ambrose saw that he was wearing an old-fashioned clerical hat, round, with a flat crown.

The clergyman's paper dropped to a lower level for a moment or two, and Ambrose, over it's brim, saw that he had on a pair of spectacles with dark, round glasses set in thick, tortoise-shell rims. The association of ideas rushed quickly to his mind. This was the very description of the Rev. James Gilbert. So it was, though, of a dozen other parsons. And Gilbert was in the Isle of Wight, with his reading party – at least, so his landlady had said yesterday.

His first impulse was to lean forward and say: "Excuse me, but are you Mr. Gilbert?" But he restrained himself. If the other was Mr. Gilbert he could not very well follow it up by questioning him on a delicate matter in the presence of the other passengers. Far better to wait till the train arrived at the London terminus and speak to him there. Even if he was not Gilbert he could scarcely ask him – whoever he was – whether he had visited St. Oswald's College between one and two on the first Tuesday in that month. No: if he spoke to him at all it must be in private.

He resumed the reading of his paper for a while. Then laid it down again and refilled and lighted his pipe. The man opposite was still intent on the Church Times. He sat, his legs crossed, and his feet stretching across the floor. Ambrose took stock of him, at least, that is, of his clothes, for his face was hidden behind the paper. The gaze of the detective-sergeant wandered downwards, along the line of waistcoat buttons showing on a dark grey suit, down his legs – to his shoes.

Ambrose knitted his brows slightly. Something was wrong – out of place. Something that jarred upon his orderly mind. What was it? Ah, yes – the metal of the clergyman's shoelaces – that was it. Those on his right foot were small, black ones, those on the left were bright and shiny – brass, and longer than the others. The laces were not a pair. As Ambrose stooped, with the ostensible purpose of knocking the ashes out of his pipe on the floor of the compartment, he could see this more plainly still. One lace was thicker than the other.

Shoelaces. Association of ideas! His mind automatically reverted to that trivial array of articles he had found in Henlow's room. Little bits of yellow earth – some cigarette ends – used matches, including the flat, red one – a broken shoelace. He had pored over them all carefully, more than once, trying to deduce some scraps of information from them. They were photographed, so to speak, on the sensitive plate of his mind.

Something, then, familiar! For, as he stooped, he saw that the brass metal tags on the left-foot shoelace were exactly similar to the one at the end of the broken lace he had found lying beside a pair of shoes in that inner room at St. Oswald's College. And one of those shoes had been devoid of a lace.

It was a remote chance to go upon, but there was a possible inference. And there was a way by which he might be able to find out if this inference was correct. That college servant – Williams. He would look after Henlow's clothes, most likely – at any rate see that his shoes were clean.

Why hadn't he thought of it before? On the first opportunity he would see Williams and ask him if he could remember if the shoes in Henlow's bedroom had their laces intact when Henlow went for his holiday. If they had, it would be quite obvious that – unless Williams had done so himself – someone must have abstracted a pair at the only time on which the rooms were accessible – the day of the committee meeting.

And on the day of that committee meeting – at the crucial hour, too, Finmere said he had seen a man of the description of the fellow sitting opposite crossing the street in front of the entrance to the college. And the fellow sitting opposite had an odd pair of laces in his shoes – and the tags of one of them tallied with that on the discarded, broken lace he had found in that bedroom!

It was plausible. The discovery, in that room, that his shoelace was broken. A hasty search for another – in the bedroom, naturally. Anyone might expect to find a few pairs of boots or shoes in a college bedroom. The hasty substitution – and then –

And then? What?

Well, there was the theory of the "invisible man." He might easily have walked out – a very familiar figure – unnoticed.

But – if this was the case, what a devilishly cool thing to do at such a time, when, in all probability, Hatton was dead in that chair.

Yes, but the murderer must have been devilishly cool. He had evidently placed the body in the chair – and arranged the open newspaper over it. And he must have kept his head precious cool, or he would never have escaped as he had done!

Ambrose returned to the perusal of his paper – perhaps more for the sake of screening himself from the man opposite than of actually reading it. He had a fresh purpose in his mind, and had no wish that the other should be too familiar with his appearance. It would never do, now, to accost him when he got out of the train. Even at the risk of postponing his interview with Sir Wilfrid Haynes he must follow up the other. Any time before two o'clock would do for that interview, so he would, at all events, have a couple of hours to spare.

The train began to run through suburban London, and Ambrose prepared to act. At length it drew up at the terminus. He let the other man get out first and followed him down the platform. A row of taxis was standing in readiness for arriving passengers, but the clergyman ignored them. At the platform barrier the detective-sergeant managed to be close behind the other as he gave up his ticket. Half a ticket. That indicated he had a return, and would be going back to Exbridge.

He followed the man out of the station to the street. There the other hailed a taxi from a stand a little way along the street. Ambrose quickly took the next one.

"I am a police sergeant," he said to the driver, showing his card. "Keep that taxi starting there in view. Sharp, now!"

"Right oh!" replied the driver, as he threw in the clutch.

The two taxis gathered speed. Ambrose took out his notebook and jotted down the registration number of the one in front. He had just time to do so when a car came out from a side street on the left and took the corner in spite of his driver's hoot. To save a collision the driver had to slacken suddenly, and the other car got in between him and his quarry. Several times he tried to pass it, but the traffic prevented him. Then came what Ambrose feared might happen. The white gauntleted arm of a policeman on point duty shot out at right-angles just as the taxi containing the clergyman had passed him – the car in front stopped in obedience to the signal.

Ambrose was out in a moment. He thrust his card under the nose of the point policeman.

"I'm after that taxi," he explained. "Let me through – quick!" and he pointed to his own taxi.

The policeman was prompt enough, but even a point policeman cannot stop a stream of cross-traffic in a moment, and the taxi in front was well on it's way – out of sight now, round a corner.

Ambrose's driver did his best. But when, in his turn, he rounded that corner, the chase had vanished. He drew up.

"Sorry!" he said, turning to his fare. "I did my best!"

"Can't be helped," replied Ambrose. "Drive to the nearest telephone now."

The nearest telephone station was a sub post office. Here, after telling his driver to wait, Ambrose rang up Scotland Yard and asked to be put on to Chief Inspector Ferguson.

"Ambrose – from Exbridge – speaking," he explained. "Do me a kindness, chief inspector . . .yes . . . it's connected with that murder case . . look here. I've just lost sight of a fellow I was anxious to trace – got away in a taxi. The taxi's number is RX1173 and he took it from the rank in Hamilton Street – just outside the terminus. Can you get hold of the driver and find out where he took his fare? Thanks very much – I'll call in this afternoon on the off-chance that you'll have the information."

He replaced the receiver and was about to leave, when a thought struck him. Consulting his notebook for a moment, he rang up again and asked to be put on to the police station at Freshwater, Isle of Wight. He had to wait some minutes before the trunk call was through. Then, explaining who he was, he gave the address provided by Mr. Gilbert's landlady.

"Find out, if you can," he said, "without arousing any suspicion, if the Reverend James Gilbert is staying there – and if he is in Freshwater today. 'Phone your reply to Chief Inspector Ferguson, Scotland Yard, and tell him it's for me."

"Now," he said, as he returned to his taxi, "drive me to the Middle Temple, please."

Directly he saw Sir Wilfrid Haynes he understood why the barrister was known to his intimate friends as "Tubby." Rotundity was his leading characteristic. He was short and stout, and his rather large face was distinctly "round." He came to the point at once, and asked Ambrose why he wanted to see him. The detective-sergeant explained that he was working on the Hatton murder case.

"Hope you'll catch the brute," said Sir Wilfrid. "Hatton was an old friend of mine. But I don't know why you've come to me. I can't help you."

"Ah, but perhaps you can, Sir Wilfrid. I imagine that Mr. Hatton paid you a visit recently."

"Yes, he did. Only a few days before his death. He dropped in to see me here. Lunched with me, in fact. How did you know he came? The usual thing, I suppose. 'From information received,' eh? That's how you police fellows put it when you want to be mysterious. Well, never mind that. He came to see me. What then?"

"Am I right in surmising that he came to ask you about something?"

The barrister slowly shook, or rather wobbled, his head.

"Not that I know of. He only called in a friendly way."

"And yet," went on Ambrose, "I have reason for surmising it was not a casual visit. Are you sure he didn't ask you any particular question, Sir Wilfrid?"

"Not that I know of. Can't remember any."

"Do you mind my asking what you talked about?"

"Not at all. Lots of things. Politics and art, and travel – and a few reminiscences of our younger days – and so on. Mere general chat."

"Nothing about whisky?"

"Whisky? What the dickens do you mean?

"I'd better explain, Sir Wilfrid. It's confidential, please?"

"That's all right. Go on."

"Well, Mr. Hatton left some curious notes – rough jottings – which I'm trying to follow up because I think they may have a reference to what happened afterwards. I've already established the fact that they bear on an important matter which I believe is connected with his death. Now these notes contain the following words – you'll forgive me being personal, Sir Wilfrid: 'Tubby's whisky. Ask him!' Followed by a line to the effect that he had seen 'Tubby.' "

The barrister laughed.

"That's my nickname – with a few old friends, right enough. My whisky, eh? What on earth – ah, I have it!"

And he brought his open palm down on the table.

"Came to ask me that, did he? Well, he did it cleverly, then. I'd no idea he was aiming at anything particular – and even now you've told me, I can't guess why. I'll tell you. Hatton and I were up at Exbridge together – not the same college. He was at Malvern. I had rooms in St. Oswald's. In the course of conversation the other day he reminded me of some of the incidents of those days – among others of a certain scout whom I strongly suspected of purloining my alcoholic drinks. My whisky dwindled too rapidly for evaporation to account for it. Well, I didn't want to make a fuss, but I managed to put a snag in the way of getting at my liquor. I've always been a bit of a carpenter. Hatton was talking about that."

"What was it?"

"In my rooms at St. Oswald's there was a bookcase – a big one that fitted in well. I bought it off my predecessor, and sold it to the man who had the rooms after me. For all I know it's there now."

"A bookcase!" exclaimed Ambrose. "This is very interesting. Please go on."

"Well, I found out that the wall behind the bookcase had a cavity – large enough to put half a dozen wine bottles in. It struck me as being a good hiding place, but of course I couldn't bother to drag the case away from the wall every time I wanted a drink. So what I did was to cut a bit out of the back of the bookcase – made a falling panel, which worked on a hinge, in point of fact. And I took a good deal of pains about it, too. I fixed it up so that, although it had no lock, no one could open it who wasn't in the secret."

"Look here, Sir Wilfrid," cried Ambrose, "did Mr. Hatton ask you to explain that secret when he came to see you the other day?"

"He didn't ask. But I did explain it. I didn't know at the time he was getting it out of me. He ought to have practised at the Bar, I can see! Clever! That was it, was it? Yes, I told him."

"What was it?"

"Quite simple when you knew it. The panel was above the third shelf – counting from the bottom, on the right. You pressed your finger against it in the centre, about three inches down from the top – and found your whisky. The panel dropped, you see. Taking it down, etc?"

For Ambrose had produced his notebook.

"No, Sir Wilfrid, I'm not taking it down. I've got it already. It's been puzzling me more than I can say. This I've copied from a bit of paper we found in the room in which Mr. Hatton was murdered, and a microscopical examination showed it had probably been in a pocket. The tiny bits of fluff we found in it were identical with the scrapings of one of Mr. Hatton's waistcoat pockets. Look at it!"

He passed the notebook to Sir Wilfrid who read:

"'3rd up – R.T. 3' down. C.' Yes, I see what you mean. The third shelf up on the right, from the top three inches down – on the centre. But what in the world has all this to do with Hatton's murder, sergeant?"

"He was seen standing in front of that bookcase very shortly before his death, studying a bit of paper. And I found out afterwards that five or six books had been removed from that particular shelf."

"Do you mean to tell me, then, that he was murdered in my old rooms?"

"Exactly."

"By George! That hadn't occurred to me. I'd no idea they were occupied by Henlow. But what does it mean, sergeant?"

"It's only conjecture, Sir Wilfrid, but I think it means that Mr. Hatton, unknowingly, was putting himself in danger. He had a suspicion that valuable stolen property was hidden in that cavity that once held your whisky, and he was putting his theory to the test – when he was interrupted."

"Who by?"

"Ah! If we knew that – !" and he broke off. "Now I want to ask you this, Sir Wilfrid. Can you think of anyone to whom you communicated the secret of that hiding place of yours?"

"Besides the man who had my rooms when I left, and to whom I sold the bookcase – who is dead now, poor chap, I never told anyone that I know of – until I mentioned it to Hatton the other day. But there was a fellow who found it out – accidentally."

"Who was that?"

"The college porter."

"The porter?"

"Yes. He came into my rooms one day – shortly before I went down – and the panel was standing open. I remember him looking at it. But the man's dead now. His nephew got the post, I think."

"His nephew? What – the present man – Bates?"

"That's the fellow."

Ambrose knit his brows in thought. He was puzzled.

"That seems to complicate matters," he said. "I don't mind telling you that the porter is under observation. But he isn't the man I'm after at the present moment."

Sir Wilfrid leaned forward over the table.

"That may be," he said. "I read the porter's evidence in the account of the inquest. I practise in criminal cases, you know, sergeant, and I'm naturally interested. And it occurred to me at the time that you have only the porter's word for checking anyone who came in or went out of the college. He may not have done the thing itself, but he may have been in collusion with someone else – someone who shared, with him, the knowledge he'd probably got from his uncle of that panel in my old bookcase. It's worth inquiring into, I think."

"I shall certainly do so."

"Meanwhile – don't answer the question if you'd rather not, but we're in the same trade, so to speak, and you can rely on me to respect your confidence. What do you imagine Hatton expected to find in that hole?"

"A Cosway miniature," replied Ambrose; "perhaps other things as well."

"Ah! I wonder if it's there now?"

"That I'll very soon find out, Sir Wilfrid; though I hardly expect it's there."

"'When she got there the cupboard was bare,' eh? Well – I'll wish you luck, sergeant. Though you may have done me out of a job!"

"How so, Sir Wilfrid?"

"Why, if you succeed in catching your man and his solicitor asked me to undertake the defence, I couldn't very well, could I? I might be wanted as a witness for the prosecution! Anyway, though, I wouldn't act for a scoundrel who'd given my old friend Hatton his quietus!"

XIV

"HALLO, sergeant!" exclaimed Chief Inspector Ferguson. "What's the parson been doing? Run away with a church collection? I've had a 'phone message for you from the station at Freshwater. Here it is," and he took up a pencilled scrap of paper. "The sergeant there says that the Reverend James Gilbert came back to his rooms this morning after having a swim. Can't you let him enjoy his holiday in peace?"

Ambrose laughed.

"Oh, that's it, is it? Yes – I won't disturb him. I'm not surprised to hear it, for I'd a good notion he wasn't the man I'm after. But how about that taxi, chief inspector? Have you traced it?"

"Yes," said Ferguson. "The report has just come in. Another parson, seemingly. Got your knife into the cloth, haven't you?"

"Where did he go?"

A smile broke out on the chief inspector's face, a sure token that he was very much interested.

"Well, my boy," he replied, "it's a funny bit of work, I fancy. You know when you came to see me before you asked me about Blaythwaite – in connection with the Hatton job. I fancy you didn't make a bad shot, after all. Though I didn't think so at the time. I told you Mrs. Blaythwaite was living at Hampstead – under another name. Well, that's where your parson johnny went in that taxi this morning – number 84 Elsworth Road."

"Good Lord!" exclaimed Ambrose, a sudden light breaking in upon him. "That's what Hatton meant in those notes of his. 'X knows the B's.' That's it."

"I'm not good at algebraic formulae," retorted Ferguson, dryly. "Perhaps you'll kindly explain. Who's X, to begin with?"

"Haven't the slightest idea – except that I've a reason for believing he's the parson in that taxi."

And he went on to explain. It was a longish story, but Ferguson listened attentively.

"Good for you!" he said, when the other had finished. "Though it's a bit of bad luck that you've lost sight of this parson. He isn't at 84 Elsworth Road now – he left before we got hold of that taxi driver."

"How do you know?"

Again the chief inspector smiled genially.

"Because we happen to be interested in the lady's movements and I've a man shadowing her. I told you we strongly suspected she's as bad as her husband, and since I saw you we've got hold of a bit or two of useful information. We want to get her on the hop – disposing of stolen goods."

"A fence?" asked Ambrose.

Ferguson nodded.

"Looks like it," he said. "My dear chap, crime isn't what it used to be when I first entered the force. It was more of a straight game then. The 'enterprising burglar went a-burgling' in the good old-fashioned way, and got rid of the goods afterwards at establishments we could keep our eyes on – more or less. In these days he's a different kind of fellow, in fact, there's no knowing at times who he is or how he disposes of the swag. And he sees he gets full value for it, often enough. He don't pick the stones out of a jewelled cup, for example, and melt the gold for the sake of the metal – if it's a question of an antique. He knows he'll get a price for it t'other side of the Atlantic from some collector who don't ask questions. And it's just here we've a notion that Mrs. Blaythwaite comes in. She seems to have a vogue for getting the goods over the water. But we'll have her! Sorry to have to postpone a happy reunion with her husband. But I hope it's going to be a case of the old cottage weather fore-teller – when the man comes out the lady goes in!"

And he laughed.

"So," he went on, "as soon as I got that taximan's story I sent to Elsworth Road, where our man's hanging about. He saw the parson go in at a few minutes past twelve and come out again in half an hour's time. And that's that. You go back to Exbridge and get on with your job, sergeant. I'll look after Mrs. Blaythwaite, and if I find out any connection between her and your murder case, I'll let you know. But you've got to be slim, my boy. On no account let that college porter suspect you know anything about that bookcase! He may not be in the racket, but don't you bet on that!"

"But – this parson –" began Ambrose.

"Keep your eyes skimmed. I'll bet my bottom dollar he's gone back to Exbridge by this time – unless," he went on, "he's stopping in town for a bit. You say he had a return ticket?"

"Not only that," replied Ambrose, "but today's our cheap return to London, and the tickets are coloured differently from the ordinary ones. His was the same colour as mine – and it's only available on the day of issue."

"Oh, go along!" chaffed the chief inspector. "Showing off, ain't you? You'll be wanting an assistant commissionership at the Yard soon at the pace you're going. All right, sergeant," he added kindly, "you're learning your job well! You ought to find the beggar in Exbridge. But take care you don't bungle matters. You want a bit more evidence for a jury than you've got yet – and, whoever 'X' may be, he's a wily chap. Look out!"

It was late in the evening when Ambrose reached Exbridge, and made his report to the superintendent. The latter, also, had news for the detective-sergeant.

"We must rule out Stanhope," he said. "He's an unshakeable alibi. He didn't much like it when I asked him to account for his movements during the luncheon hour, but he came round when I showed him it was to his own advantage to do so. Well, he comes out of it all right. He lunched at Simpkin's – the Bell restaurant, you know, in West Street, and was there till after two o'clock. Simpkin and the head waiter – both of whom know him – corroborated this. Then he bought some tobacco at Slater's shop – and I satisfied myself on that point. Then I went to see Wilkins, the clerk at the insurance office opposite St. Oswald's, on the off-chance that he might have spotted him out of the window. He did. Recognised the description. Saw him come up to the college a little before half-past two and stand just within the entrance lighting his pipe – when Kershaw joined him and they both went in together."

The detective-sergeant's report of his day's work prompted the superintendent to telephone to the chief constable, asking if he were at home – which he was. Both men immediately went round to his house, and a long consultation followed. As a result it was determined that steps should be taken for a diligent search in Exbridge for the individual answering to the description of the clergyman who had travelled to London with Ambrose, and that the next morning, Ambrose should call on Mr. Henlow, take him into his confidence, and probe the secret – if any – of the bookcase.

Finally Ambrose went to his rooms rather tired, and quite ready for his supper. He was greeted, as he came into the house, by his landlady's little girl.

"Hallo, Muriel," he said; "not gone to bed yet?"

"Daddy took me to the pictures tonight – and we've only just got home. Oh, Mr. Ambrose, I did so want to ask you about that postcard you sent me. May I bring it to you?"

"All right," replied Ambrose, "if mummy doesn't mind."

"Don't worry Mr. Ambrose now, Muriel," said her mother, appearing from the back room. "It's time you were in bed."

"Please, mummy!"

"Oh, let her come in while I have my supper, Mrs. Glover. I won't let her stay long."

The child rushed off to get the postcard, returning with it to Ambrose's room.

"Well," said that good-natured young man, "what do you want to know about it, Muriel?"

"I want you to tell me what the words mean – and what the picture's about."

"Get a chair, then, and sit down by me. That's it." He put the card on the table. "Now this is a picture of a great big piece of water – "

"Like the sea, Mr. Ambrose?"

"No, not quite like the sea. Not so large, you know – and the water isn't salt, like the sea. It's called a lake."

"Oh, yes, I know. We learn about lakes in school."

"Yes, well, this is a very beautiful lake, with big mountains round parts of it – some of them have snow in their tops all the year round."

"In summer?"

"Yes, even in summer. It's very cold up on the top, you see, and the snow doesn't melt."

"What's the name of the lake, Mr. Ambrose?"

"We generally call it the Lake of Geneva, because there's a big town named Geneva, at one end of it. But out there they call it Lake Leman."

"Does it say so in those funny words?"

"Not exactly. Look now: I'll tell you what they mean. We'll have a lesson in French."

He pointed to the inscription, translating it word for word.

"'EVIAN-LES-BAINS,' that's the name of the place where I bought it. Evian is the name of the town, and because people go there to drink a funny kind of water, and have baths they call it Evian Baths – 'LES BAINS' is French for 'the baths.' 'QUAY DES BATTEAUX.' – that means the landing place where the steamboats come – they've got big steamers on the lakes; and this picture is a photograph taken from the quay, or landing stage. 'VUE DE LAC ET LA SUISSE.' That's 'view of the lake and Switzerland.' On the opposite side of the lake it's Switzerland, you see, but Evian is in France."

"Oh! I understand now, Mr. Ambrose. But what does this say, please?"

And the child pointed with her finger to some minute lettering in the left-hand bottom corner of the postcard.

Ambrose read out loud:

"'JEAN NATIER, PHOT., EVIAN-LES-BAINS.' Oh, that's the name of the man who took the photograph. 'John Natier, photographer, Evian of the Baths.' That's nothing to do with the picture, Muriel."

"Come along, dear!" exclaimed her mother, who came into the room with a tray of dishes at that moment. "Say goodnight to Mr. Ambrose, and go straight up to bed now."

The child took up her postcard.

"Thank you ever so much, Mr. Ambrose. Goodnight."

"Goodnight, Muriel."

Ambrose, left alone to his supper, ate it rather slowly, in spite of his appetite. He was thinking. Something about those words he had translated last seemed familiar, but, for the life of him, he could remember no connection. 'JEAN NATIER.' Where had he come across a photographer of that name?

He gave it up, finished his supper, and consoled himself with his pipe.

But, over and over again, the name rose in his mind.

"Jean Natier!"

XV

"I WANT to ask you rather a curious question," said Ambrose to Williams, the college servant, the next morning; "but before I do so I should like to have your assurance that you won't mention it to anyone."

"I understand, sergeant. I know how to keep my mouth shut."

"For the present," went on Ambrose, "I don't want the subject of my question to get about. That's all. I shall be explaining it to Mr. Henlow presently, but, apart from you and him it's important that no one else should get wind of it. Now then, I suppose you see to Mr. Henlow's clothes, don't you?"

"Yes – in a way. I brush them, and so on."

"Exactly. And clean his shoes, eh?"

"No, I don't do that. I only take them from his rooms to be cleaned."

"Oh, well – that's quite enough. Now, when he went away on his holiday he left a few pairs of shoes behind, didn't he? In the bottom of that wardrobe in his bedroom?"

"Yes, he did. I don't know how you guessed that, sergeant."

"I didn't guess it. It was my business to make a thorough search – and I noticed the shoes were there. Now, can you tell me if one shoe had no lace in it when he went for his holiday?"

"It's a funny thing you should ask me that," replied Williams. "I suppose you must have seen one of 'em had no lace in it?"

"I did. That's why I'm asking you."

"Well, now, sergeant, I never noticed it till the day Mr. Henlow came back. I was unpacking his suitcase and putting his things away – shoes among the rest – when I happened to glance at one of the pairs in that wardrobe. One shoe, as you say, had no lace in it. I took the shoes away to put in a new pair of laces – and mentioned it to Mr. Henlow at the time. But why I say it's a funny thing is because I could have sworn that when I saw those shoes last – just before Mr. Henlow went away – they had both laces, all right. And I know Mr. Henlow didn't wear that particular pair for at least a week before he left."

"Oh!" exclaimed Ambrose, "that's very interesting. Thanks. That's all I want to know now. I'll go and see Mr. Henlow – if he's in."

"He isn't in his rooms just now, sergeant. I think he's in the library. I saw him go in there about half an hour ago."

"All right. Take me to the library, please."

The detective-sergeant found Henlow deeply immersed in a bulky volume he had taken from one of the shelves.

"I'm sorry to disturb you, sir. I'm detective-sergeant Ambrose of the Exbridge police, and I'm investigating the case of Mr. Hatton's death. Can you spare me a few minutes?"

Henlow looked at him sharply.

"Certainly. What can I do for you?"

"Would you mind if we went to your rooms, sir? I'd rather talk to you there, if I might."

"Oh – certainly, if you wish it. Come along."

He led the way through some passages, across the small inner quad, to his rooms up the staircase in the corner, Ambrose following him. The two armchairs were on either side of the fireplace. Henlow sat down in one of them and motioned Ambrose to take the other. Then he took a case from his pocket and extracted a cigarette.

"Well, what do you want to ask me? Do you smoke?"

And he offered the open cigarette case to the detective-sergeant.

"Thank you, sir. I've come on an extremely confidential errand – you will understand?"

And he lighted his cigarette. Henlow did the same with his.

"Quite so."

"There are several matters, sir, apparently connected with this case . . ."

He stopped short. In throwing down his half-burnt match it had fallen on the hearth rug instead of into the grate. He stooped to pick it up – and chucked it into the fire.

A very natural action, ostensibly. But a quickly conceived one in order to give himself a moment's breathing space. For Ambrose had suddenly realised – in a flash – that never, in the whole of his police career, had he had need to be complete master of himself as he had at that moment, never had he had cause to think more clearly, or to hide his thoughts.

In one glance he had seen something – something that might have made a man with less self-control give vent to a startled ejaculation, and what he had seen was this:

Henlow was seated in the chair opposite, in an easy attitude, one leg crossed over the other. He was wearing a dark brown jacket and trousers. In leaning forward to light his cigarette Ambrose happened to glance downwards. It may have been that the detective-sergeant's subconscious mind had registered a similar action on his part the day before, and thus rendered him susceptible to its continuous repetition. For, as he afterwards declared, that casual downward glance brought, at once, the thought of shoelaces before his mind.

And there they were too! The pair of laces in Henlow's shoes were not a pair. They did not match. One was distinctly thicker than the other, and while one had black metal tags on its ends, the other tags were bright brass ones – brass ones, similar to those he had studied and thought about so carefully.

In emergencies there often seems no time-limit to thoughts – they sometimes rush with amazing rapidity through the brain in the space of a couple of seconds. They did now. Impossible! Henlow, the staid Professor of Greek – Fellow of his college – stiff, even severe. The typical Exbridge don! Impossible.

"Impossible!" That was the word Hatton had jotted down in those queer notes of his.

"Impossible!" Henlow had been in Switzerland when the murder had taken place.

And yet – the coincidence stared him in the face. Those two odd shoelaces! What it all meant he could not grasp at the moment, but one thing he did see – at once! He would have to be cautious. At all costs he must steer clear of the two topics which were the basis of his visit – the shoelaces, and the hiding place behind the books.

With perfectly admirable nonchalance he slowly raised himself from his stooping position, sat back in his chair, blew out a little cloud of cigarette smoke, and went on from the point where he had broken off.

" – matters which may seem insignificant, but which may have a bearing of importance."

"Yes?" replied Henlow. "What are they?"

Ambrose was almost stumped. But his quick, inventive brain saved him. One more little breathing space, as he took a pull at his cigarette – how he blessed that cigarette! – and he said:

"Well, sir, in confidence, I'd like to ask you a few questions about Williams."

"Do you suspect him, then?"

Ambrose shrugged his shoulders.

"I don't say that. But I'm not altogether satisfied with his evidence."

"Hasn't he an alibi to the effect that he could not have been in this room when the crime was committed?"

Henlow asked the question coldly enough. But his eyes were fixed on the detective-sergeant's face and Ambrose felt, instinctively, that the question was a very probing one.

"That may be," he replied, "but you can't always put your trust in alibis. People may, innocently enough, think they are quite certain as to a particular time or event, but memory of trivialities is sometimes shaky. Have you known him long, sir?"

"Several years."

"And his character?"

"Quite exemplary."

Ambrose, by this time, had pulled out his notebook. References to it formed opportunities for slight pauses – for thought.

"He said," he went on, "that there was only one key to your rooms – and that you left it with him."

"Quite right. He foolishly lost his in the river. There are two keys now. I've had a duplicate made."

"I see."

Ambrose grew more confident in himself. It was less of an effort now to avoid dangerous subjects. He went on, asking various questions – about Williams – the members of the committee – the procedure at their meetings, and so forth. But he never once mentioned the clergyman who had been seen approaching the college – never asked Henlow if anyone of that description was in the habit of coming to his rooms.

And as he went on talking his thoughts became clearer – and shaped themselves into a definite plan.

He got up, at length, to go, and thanked the other for the interview, apologising for having taken up his time.

"Not at all," replied Henlow. "I'm only too glad to have been of any use – if I have!"

And again he looked keenly at the detective-sergeant. But the latter only glanced at his notebook, and replaced it in his pocket.

At the gate of the college he accosted the porter.

"You've a telephone in your lodge, haven't you? Right. I want to use it for a moment – no, you needn't bother to come in – I'll manage."

He rang up the superintendent, and sank his voice very low when the reply came.

"Got anyone in plain clothes at the station, sir?"

"Yes. Jackson."

"Will you please send him to St. Oswald's College at once, sir – and tell him to hang about outside and keep an eye on Mr. Henlow if he comes out."

"Henlow?" The superintendent's voice rang with surprise.

"I'll explain presently, sir. I've got a call to make, and then I'll be with you. If Henlow should leave the town, Jackson must follow him."

Outside the college he had a word with a policeman on point-duty.

"Just till Jackson comes," he explained. And the constable, leaving the traffic to look after itself, moved along the street and took up a position near the college entrance. Ambrose hailed a taxi, and gave the driver directions – which was the residence of Dr. Blake.

In that short taxi journey he had a little breathing space to think out matters. He saw the two chief difficulties – difficulties, that is, which lay in the way of any decisive proof which would convince a jury that Henlow was guilty – not only of Hatton's murder, but of crime which led to that murder. Could he find any reason which suggested that Henlow had disguised himself as a weak-eyed parson, and could he produce any evidence suggesting that Henlow was not at Geneva when Hatton was killed? Three things he had in his mind, and the third thing, that fragment of a red match, rested on the second. Two witnesses, so to speak, for the prosecution – the Professor of Divinity and little Muriel Glover – two witnesses, both of whom, quite unconsciously, had given him the two clues which were in his mind.

The professor was in his study when Ambrose was shown in.

"Ah, young man! You again, eh? What is it? I can only spare you a few minutes. I've an appointment at half-past eleven."

"I won't detain you long, sir. You remember telling me how you met a friend at Cromer when you were wearing

217

dark glasses, and a lay hat and collar, and that he failed to recognise you?"

"Quite right. What about it?"

"Who was he, professor?"

"Who was he? Why – dear me, what a queer question! If you want to know he was Mr. Sidney Henlow."

"I knew it!" exclaimed Ambrose, triumphantly. "Thank you very much, sir – you've done me a great service."

"Here – come back!" cried the professor, as Ambrose made for the door. "What conjuring trick are you up to now, young man? I want to know – "

"Sorry, sir, but I haven't a moment to spare. I'll explain some day – good morning!"

He was off before the professor could get in another word. He told his taximan to drive to the police station – and wait there. Arrived at the station he made a dash for his office and unlocked a drawer in his desk, and produced a number of articles which he had collected in Henlow's room. But only one of them seemed to interest him, and that was the postcard with the Swiss stamp and Geneva post-mark which Henlow had sent to Pennington, stating that he would not be home for the committee meeting. It was a picture postcard, and Henlow had written his brief communication on the space provided in front, side by side with the space for the address.

Ambrose turned it over. It was a view of the southern end of the lake, with mountains in the background, evidently taken from a steamer or boat. The inscription was:

"LE DENT DU MIDI,"

But it was not this inscription which Ambrose read with interest. His gaze fell on some words in minute lettering at the corner of the card.

"JEAN NATIER. PHOT. EVIAN-LES-BAINS."

"Eureka!" he ejaculated. "'Out of the mouths of babes —'" and hurried to the superintendent's room.

"You see, sir," he explained, after recounting his interview with Henlow that morning and the suspicion aroused by the shoelaces, "this is how I figured it – and I think I'm right. Henlow and that parson are one and the same man. He got the idea of a simple but effective disguise, from Dr. Blake. The professor had told me how he once wore dark sunglasses and an ordinary tie and collar and panama hat at Cromer, and how a man he knew well had come face to face with him without recognising him. And he's just told me that man was Henlow. Well, Henlow evidently caught the idea, but reversed the disguise – with the exception of the spectacles."

"How do you mean he reversed it?"

"Why, Dr. Blake, as a parson, was taken for a layman. Henlow, as a layman, passed as a cleric. The round hat and the collar were all he wanted. It's a very common disguise in a town like this, you see. There are lots of similar parsons – one Mr. Gilbert, who was in the habit of visiting Henlow in his rooms. So it was quite possible for him to go in and out of the college unnoticed as Henlow."

"Yes – but why?"

"Because he's 'X,' sir. I'm pretty sure of that. And so was that poor chap Hatton. That's why he was done in."

"But Henlow was abroad!"

"No, sir! Not a bit of it. The parson whom Mr. Finmere saw making for the college was Henlow all the time."

"But, how could he be?"

"Because everything points to it, sir. That half-burnt match has given him away. It must have come from Evian-les-Bains. It's the only place where one can get them. I proved that."

"But he posted a card from Geneva."

"Exactly. But he bought it at Evian-les-Bains all the same. Here it is, sir. Look at the name of the local photographer on it. An Evian photographer. I ought to have spotted it before now, only I hadn't attached any importance to the card. I bought one of the same series when I was at Evian. He may have posted it at Geneva, but they'd hardly sell French postcards there. He got it when he stayed at Evian – and we'll have to prove he was there. That's easily done. A matter of hotel registers."

"But if all this is as you say, I'm still puzzled, sergeant. Why the deuce should he take the trouble to go to his own rooms in disguise – and on a day when he knew that committee would be sitting there?"

"I've figured that out, roughly, sir. He probably wanted to get something out of that room and run no risk of anyone knowing he had been there. And his only chance of getting into his rooms unobserved was on that Tuesday. Williams held the only key. But he knew the door would be unlocked during the luncheon hour, and calculated the room would be empty – as it always was on such an occasion. It wasn't empty. Hatton was there. And Hatton had just probed the secret of those stolen goods – he'd been on the track for weeks. And Henlow couldn't afford to let him spread the news."

The superintendent pondered.

"I believe there's something in it," he said at length. "We've enough to act upon, anyhow. But, if all you say is correct, how did he manage to get out of the college? Tell me that, Ambrose!"

Ambrose shook his head.

"I can't, sir. That stumps me, I admit. Unless the porter failed to notice him like the invisible man in one of Chesterton's stories, you know, sir – because he was too familiar a sight."

The superintendent grinned.

"I don't believe in the story books, Ambrose – and I'm not going to accept that theory. But now, we won't lose any time. Lucky there's no need for a warrant for an arrest for murder. You and I will go at once and bring him along."

"I thought you would, sir. I've a taxi ready outside. We don't want to march him along the High Street."

"We'll have to be a bit careful," said the superintendent, as they started in the taxi. "I won't charge him to begin with.

We'll just ask him to come to the station, and have a word or two with him first."

The taxi entered the High Street and approached the college. As they came near the detective-sergeant suddenly exclaimed.

"By George, sir! There's a taxi at the gate! Surely..."

"Damn!" broke in the superintendent. "Why doesn't that fool Jackson stop him? He's got in – he's off, the beggar!"

For they had seen Henlow come quickly out of the gate and enter the waiting taxi. Jackson, lounging about at the entrance, had made a sudden move towards it, but too late. The driver had thrown in the clutch and started. The taxi moved across the street to take the left-hand side, crossing in front of them.

The superintendent put his head out of the window and shouted to the other driver, but, at that moment, a big lorry came between the two vehicles, and the man did not see or hear him. The superintendent cried to his own driver:

"Swing her round – quick, man – and follow that taxi! D'you hear?"

"Right, sir!"

He swung round, slowly, then gathered speed. The other taxi was still in view.

The superintendent heaved a sigh of relief.

"That's all right," he said. "Lucky we came up just when we did. He can't get away very well now. Ah – I thought so. Making for the railway station! We'll have him there."

Ambrose looked at his watch.

"It's a near go," he exclaimed. "He's evidently after the twelve-fifteen express to town. It's thirteen minutes past now."

"Even if he gets it before we can catch him we'll have him," retorted the other, grimly. "Thank God for the telephone! Go on!" he yelled to the driver, putting his head outside the window again.

The actual approach to the station was a broad road, widening out into a large open space in front of the entrance. They were only fifty yards or so behind as the first taxi drew up at the entrance. Henlow had the door open before it stopped. They saw him jump out, thrust something into the driver's hand, and bolt into the station. In less than half a minute they followed – rushing on to the platform. There was a hiss of steam – the train was just coming in. The platform was crowded with passengers.

The superintendent had just time for a word with the ticket collector at the barrier.

"Don't let anyone through!" he cried. "Yes – a police job," and the man closed and locked the gate.

A hasty word to a railway inspector on the platform – orders quickly given by him to porters and guard, and the superintendent tapped Ambrose on the shoulder.

"Let 'em all get in," he said, "and we'll go through the train. Haven't spotted him, have you?"

"No."

"Don't worry. He can't get away now. And he had no time to take a ticket – there were three others at the window of the booking-office when we came in – ah, good-morning, station-master – I want your help."

It was all done very systematically. Ambrose stationed himself at the barrier, scrutinising all who went out. The platform was cleared. A porter ran along the train locking all the doors. Two others had already performed the same office on the other side of the train. There were no means of escaping across the line. Then the superintendent, accompanied by the station-master and a ticket collector – the latter ostensibly examining all tickets – entered every compartment in turn while the inspector and a guard walked through the corridor, and searched the lavatories.

All in vain. There was not the slightest sign of Henlow on the train, and, reluctantly, the superintendent had to agree that it might start.

But he had not finished his search. A couple of policemen, telephoned for, came up, and every nook and cranny of the station was examined – again in vain.

The ticket collector at the barrier was sharply questioned, and declared that no one had passed him without a ticket. All with train tickets? Well, no – people had come on the platform to see their friends off. He produced the platform tickets they had given up when they went out. How many had come on? That he really couldn't say – he hadn't counted them. The platform tickets were had, of course, from that penny-in-the-slot machine close by – in the booking office.

And then Ambrose had a sudden idea. He ran down the steps leading off the platform to the subway, crossed to the down platform, and for the second time, interrogated the ticket collector at the barrier there. The man had already told him that a train had left the down platform just as the up express was coming in, but that no one had passed out of his gate without a ticket.

"Look here," said Ambrose, "did anyone come on from the down booking-office here with a platform ticket?"

"Only one lady, I'm certain of that."

"Let me see all the tickets you collected from the outgoing passengers – ah – I guessed right, then! You've two platform tickets here, my man! We've got to thank you for letting him slip through."

"How was I to know, guv'nor?"

"You couldn't, I admit."

He went back to the superintendent on the other platform.

"He's not here," he explained. "He'd just time to get a platform ticket. He evidently saw it was too late for the train, so he ran down the subway – and got out the other side while we were searching for him here."

"Damn!" exclaimed the superintendent. "We've wasted time, then. I must warn all stations now – and have an eye kept on all roads out of Exbridge. Let's get to it!"

But in spite of all precaution, in spite of careful inquiries in Exbridge itself, no reports came in that day – or ever afterwards. In some way or other Henlow had shown a clean pair of heels.

Later on that day the chief constable, the superintendent, and Ambrose were closeted together in the room that had been the scene of the crime. The detective-sergeant had a scrap of paper in his hand. He removed a row of books from one of the shelves of the bookcase, and pressed his thumb on the panel at the back, in the centre, about three inches down from the top. There was a sharp "click," and removing his hand from it, the panel, hinged at the bottom, fell forward, flat on the shelf, disclosing a cavity in the wall behind.

"Now!" exclaimed Colonel Langdale, "what are we going to find, I wonder? That is, if Henlow's left anything. Go on, sergeant – you made the discovery. Show us!"

Ambrose put his arm into the cavity, felt downwards, and withdrew it with a brown paper roll in his hand, a roll about three feet in length, tied up with string. He cut the string, removed the brown paper, and unrolled a canvas, holding it up to the light – a picture of a landscape, with a group in the foreground.

"Jove!" cried the colonel. "Exhibit one. That's the lost 'Corot.' The Provost of Malvern won't be sorry to have it back. Anything else, Ambrose?"

"Dr. Blake's Cosway, I hope – he deserves to get it back from the help he's given us. Hallo – what's this?"

"Exhibit two!" said the chief constable, grimly. "Take care how you handle it, Ambrose. We may want fingerprints."

"All right, sir. I haven't touched the hilt."

He laid it, gingerly, on the table. Jewels sparkled in the gold hilt of a small dagger, sheathed in a beautifully embossed leather sheath, tipped, also, with gold. Very carefully, holding down the hilt to the table with the back of the blade of his penknife, he drew off the sheath, disclosing an exquisitely chased blade about six inches in length, keen-edged and sharply pointed. The superintendent bent over it, shrugged his shoulders, and pointed to a brown smudge near the hilt.

The chief constable nodded.

"That's it," he said. "We must have it analysed, of course. But there doesn't seem to be much doubt about it, does there?"

"I've sometimes wondered whether all Mr. Finmere told us about that paper-knife was O.K.," remarked the superintendent. "But I'll give him the credit now of speaking the truth. Anything else, sergeant?"

"I'd better look first. Your warning about fingerprints," he went on to the chief constable, "reminded me that I've been a bit clumsy."

He drew a small electric torch from his pocket and flashed it into the cavity.

"Not a thing!" he said. "It's quite empty now. I'm sorry. I should have liked to have taken that miniature back to the professor – and delighted him with another conjuring trick," he added, beneath his breath.

The only other finds of any interest were in a small suitcase, the lock of which Ambrose picked with a skeleton key selected from a small bunch he carried. They were a round, black, low-crowned hat, a clerical collar and stock, and a pair of tortoiseshell spectacles with large, darkly-tinted glasses.

XVI

"You have heard," said the coroner at the adjourned inquest, "statements which are extraordinary, even in a court which is accustomed to elicit at times surprising evidence. Before calling upon you to record your verdict I should like to make a few remarks upon these statements.

"In the first place, then, I am sure you will agree with me that Mr. Finmere is exonerated from all complicity with the death of Mr. Hatton, while, at the same time, you will, doubtless, congratulate him on being extricated from a most unpleasant situation. I mean that if ever there was a case in which circumstantial evidence appeared to point with unwavering finger it is this. Mr. Finmere was seen to be with Mr. Hatton a very short time before the latter's death, he had had occasion to quarrel with him, and – he must not mind my saying so – is known to be a man of violent temper and hasty impulse. Moreover, to all appearance, he was the only individual who could have entered and left that room in St. Oswald's College, within that very short time-limit which was essential to the accomplishment of the crime. Again, the weapon with which to all human appearances Mr. Hatton was killed lay on the table in that room – ready to hand. Further, Mr. Finmere left the country immediately – at the earliest opportunity. It is true that his visit to the artist in St. John's Wood and what he told that artist about his interview with Mr. Hatton, might have been taken as evidence of his innocence. But not necessarily. Many a man who has committed a crime gives himself away by some explanatory excuse afterwards – an excuse which has its origin in the fear of the real facts being discovered. Even when he voluntarily made the statement that he had thrown the knife away – that was no proof that he had not first made use of it as a weapon of attack.

"The public is sometimes inclined to criticise the police as blunderers. It would have been a tremendous blunder if the police, in this instance, had ignored all other possibilities and narrowed down their investigations to the line which appeared to be the most plausible. But here you have an instance of that meticulous care with which the police are not always credited. Not satisfied with merely pursuing the most obvious theory they broadened their investigations with an open mind, and took into consideration every inference – even the apparently most trivial ones – which seemed to be in any way connected with the case. The result, you will probably admit, is extraordinary, though I will not anticipate your verdict by citing it. But I do ask you, in arriving at that verdict, to take into consideration the chain of evidence which has been submitted in this inquiry. A bit of a broken shoelace – a half-burnt match – an evening newspaper – half a sheet of notepaper with a cryptic inscription upon it – the chance utterance by a university professor of a friend failing to recognise him on account of a slight change of attire – and so forth.

"Whether you are of the opinion that the following up of these items and the connection between them points emphatically to the individual at whose hands Mr. Hatton met his death is for you to say. It is a question of inference. The police themselves, though they have, I suppose, no doubt in their own minds will admit this. Even the fact of the individual in question having eluded arrest is no conclusive proof in itself that he is guilty. There is rarely direct evidence in a crime of this nature. None the less, justice, over and over again, has been satisfied not by direct evidence, but from inferences.

"One other point I would mention before I ask you to record your verdict. This inquiry has taken us beyond the actual death of Mr. Hatton into a realm of crime with which the police hold it was closely connected – was, in fact, the result of those other crimes. The police have presented you with a drama, the leading character of which, so they contend, played more than one part. Preposterous as this may, perhaps, appear to you, unfortunately the history of humanity teems with such dual characteristics, and, over and over again, the most subtle, the most dangerous, and often the most successful criminal is not the person who poses to the world as such, but the man who conceals his criminal tendencies under the cloak of the role he publicly plays before the world. I will now ask you to record, in the form of your verdict, your considered opinion of the cause by which this unfortunate man was killed."

And, after quite a brief consultation, the foreman of the jury announced their verdict:

"We find that Francis Hatton met with his death at the hands of Sidney Henlow."

"Which," said the coroner, "amounts to a verdict of wilful murder?"

"That is what we mean, sir."

"And I agree with you. That concludes this inquiry. I should like to add, before I close the court, that I trust the police will be successful in bringing what arises out of the verdict – and their own investigations – before another court, which, unlike this, has the issues of life and death under its control!"

XVII

PERHAPS two letters will form the best conclusion to the Hatton murder case – that is, as far as it might be said to be ever concluded.

I. – Letter from Chief Inspector Ferguson, of the C.I.D. to Detective-Sergeant Ambrose, of the Exbridgeshire Police.

"Private.

"DEAR AMBROSE, – I was sorry to find when I paid an official visit to Exbridge last week, that you were fishing out something or other at the other end of the county, for I should have liked to have congratulated you personally on your handling of the Hatton case. Pity you made a bungle of it at the end, though! You were a bit too cautious, my boy. What you ought to have done as soon as you suspected Henlow was to have got him to go with you to the police station, on some excuse or other, and to have kept him there while you made those final inquiries that clinched the matter.

You might have been pretty sure that so wily a bird might have suspected your visit to him the day after you travelled with him in the train, for, no doubt, he recognised you as his fellow passenger. I didn't, however, put this view of the case to that good-looking superintendent of yours who, you will be glad to know, looks on you as a smart lad, which means, I hope, a rise.

"But I'm not writing this to criticise you. That's only by the way. I thought you'd like to hear about Mrs. Blaythwaite – or Mrs. Harford, as she called herself when she went to live in Elsworth Road. I told you we were keeping an eye on her, and Henlow's visit to her in his round hat and goggles only increased our vigilance.

"Now, for over a year we've had cause to suspect the movements of two men – Americans – who have been constantly crossing to and fro from New York, apparently on business (and it was business, too – of a kind). These fellows never came over together, but they stayed – when they came – at the same hotel here, and we got to know that a certain individual we have reason (but no proof, unfortunately) to believe is a fence where stolen articles of intrinsic value are concerned, visited each of them. Their names (or, at any rate, the names they went by) were James B. Higgins and Morton H. Stockwell respectively.

"Stockwell was in England a few weeks ago. As a matter of fact he sailed for New York on the day that Hatton was murdered – took the night boat-train from Waterloo. Higgins turned up about ten days afterwards – and posted a letter in the hotel letter-box addressed to Mrs. Harford. We had an inkling all along that she was in communication with them.

"So we watched. To make a long story short Mrs. Blaythwaite met Higgins on Primrose Hill – which is close by her house. It was an artful arrangement. You know the hill is an open space with paths intersecting it, and seats about. She sat down on one of these seats and presently Higgins came sauntering along the path and sat down at the other end of it. Apparently there was no communication between them, but our two men behind some shrubs in the background saw her push something along the seat towards him – and a vice versa action on his part. A civil, but rather insistent inquiry immediately afterwards brought to light a small parcel in Higgins' overcoat pocket and a nice little wad of Bank of England notes in the lady's vanity bag – notes which we afterwards proved to have been some of a number paid out by a bank in exchange for a cheque in dollars bearing the signature of a well-known financier at Brooklyn, U.S.A., who is an ardent collector of antiques, and, apparently is not too particular as to how he collects them. (Pity we can't touch him – but there's not sufficient proof. The cheque was a 'bearer' one.) The particular antique in question was a snuff-box with a miniature on it!

"With equal civility and insistence the pair of them was invited to pay a visit to Scotland Yard – and are still enjoying His Majesty's hospitality pending the opportunity of an interview with one of His Majesty's judges.

"In Higgins' room at his hotel we found a pretty little assortment of curios, some of which we recognised as being particularly wanted by their late owners. With regard to this particular miniature, however, I remembered what you had told me about Hatton's investigation. I also remembered the visit of the parson to Mrs. Blaythwaite. So I ran down to Exbridge, paid a preliminary visit to your super, and then called on that rather voluble professor about whom you had told me. He was delighted to recognise his 'Cosway,' as he called it, but it took me a little time to explain to the old blighter that he couldn't have it then and there, because we wanted it as 'Exhibit No.I' at the trial. By the way, he told me you were good at conjuring tricks. What was he driving at?

"Mrs. Blaythwaite is as dumb as an oyster. I fancy she could throw a good deal of light on your murder case, but she won't, my boy! Anyhow I think we've scotched, for a while, her little game of acting as an intermediary for Yankee collectors of objects of art. And I don't suppose Morton H. Stockwell will be crossing the herring pond for some little time. I wish we'd got him, too!

"When you apply for the assistant commissionership here, don't forget old friends, but deal mercifully with the slips and failures of

"Yours sincerely,

"HARRY FERGUSON."

II. – Letter from Sidney Henlow to the Chief Constable of Exbridgeshire. (Six months later.)

"MY DEAR LANGDALE, – If you fondly imagine that the postmark on the envelope containing this letter will be of any use to you, I had better begin by saying it will not. I am, as you will rightly conjecture, 'somewhere in the world,' but this letter will not be posted in that particular 'somewhere.'

"I have, for some time, had it in my mind to write to you. I do not wish to make any sentimental excuses for what has happened; but I should like one of those who were my friends to know some of the circumstances which led to an action which I shall never cease deeply to regret – though I am still disinclined to pay the penalty which the law demands for its commission. And I have selected you as the recipient of my confidences because, associated so closely as you are with criminology, your judgment may not be so hard as that of those to whom such a crime as mine can never be understood because they have never been tempted to commit one. I know very little about the police, but sufficient to have observed that, though they wage war with crime, they are often very human in their attitude towards the criminal.

"I propose, therefore, without, as I have said, indulging in sentiment or endeavouring to whitewash myself, to recount, very briefly, the course of events which led to the tragedy enacted in my rooms, and to give you an explanation – which I think is due to certain officers under your command – of how I managed to elude discovery on the actual day of poor Hatton's death, and how, finally, I made my escape from Exbridge.

"R. L. Stevenson in the *Strange Case of Dr. Jekyll and Mr. Hyde* might, with truth, have left the word 'strange' out of the title, for dual personality is not so uncommon. Most

men have two sides to their nature, and the theological
doctrine of original sin contending with righteousness is true
all through the ages in its biological aspect. Fortunately,
perhaps, for humanity one nature usually predominates in
the individual, and the Dr. Jekylls do not alternate with the
Mr. Hydes in any marked degree.

"I suppose, though, that I was one of the exceptions.
You knew me as a staid university don, but I was led, also, to
play the part which your very astute detective-sergeant
discovered.

"Financial difficulties were at the root of it. I speculated
– and often lost. My emoluments and the meagre amount I
made from my books, were insufficient to cover my losses. I
will not inculpate others by giving you the details of how I
became acquainted with a man and a woman who showed
me a means of making money without much effort – I
suppose you would call them 'crooks.' They were in touch
with agents who supplied unscrupulous American collectors
with European objects of art, objects which had necessarily,
to be concealed by their ultimate purchasers, who were
content, with that strange craving to possess which lies at the
root of the collector's infatuation, to hold them in secret.

"These two persons were, themselves, purloiners of
other people's goods – the man was caught, and paid the
penalty. Imprisonment. Afterwards, his wife put certain
propositions before me, dilating on the fact that my position
enabled me to acquire, without suspicion, certain objects –
publicly or privately possessed – which were coveted.

"So I fell. It began with the Warmingham Missal, in the possession of the library at Maxham. I walked out of the library one day with the Missal in my despatch case – and was afterwards the richer by a considerable sum. Then there was the Etruscan Vase, missing from the Brendon Museum. With a similar result.

"I had to be very cautious, however, and I began to see that if I was to continue in my new career it would never do for me to run the risk of possibly being observed near the scene of crime, or in dealing with the intermediary. I happened to meet a clerical friend, on his holiday, who had discarded clerical hat and collar for lay attire, and was wearing dark glasses as a protection from the sun, and I failed to recognise him, even at close quarters, until he jocularly made himself known to me. I reversed the process by turning myself into a bespectacled clergyman at will. It was easy to carry a rolled-up soft hat, a collar and a pair of glasses. An ordinary dark grey suit did the rest.

"Moreover the disguise was a very common one. Exbridge abounded in such parsons, and one of them occasionally visited me in my rooms. I was able, when caution demanded it, to go in and out of the college unrecognised. I was able to make my way to London and dispose of certain articles without rousing suspicion as to my real personality.

"With regard to these 'certain articles,' they could only be disposed of when definite opportunities arose. My ally in London absolutely refused to take the risk of harbouring them in her house for any length of time. She fixed the exact date on which I was to take them to her, and, I suppose, got rid of them, in her turn, on the same day. So I had to provide a secure hiding place in my rooms. That was easily done as, of course, you know. I had the secret of that panel in the bookcase from the last occupant of the rooms.

"These preliminaries will suffice to bring my story to a head. When I started abroad for my holiday there were three very valuable objects in the cavity behind that bookcase, one of them the 'Corot,' which was missing from the Provost of Malvern. My London ally knew of this 'Corot,' and was taking steps to get rid of it for me. Before leaving, I gave her my address – an hotel at Evian-les-Bains, little thinking what would be the result.

"I spent a fortnight at Evian-les-Bains, and then went on to Geneva, by boat. On the journey I remembered that the Consultative Committee was due to meet at my rooms on the following Tuesday. I happened to have a postcard on me, and wrote, with a fountain pen, to the secretary of the committee, to the effect that I should not be back, but that the room would be available, and the first thing I did on arrival at an hotel at Geneva was to write a letter to Williams, instructing him to make the usual preparations. Both letter and card were posted in Geneva.

"I had left my new address at the Evian hotel. Two days afterwards a letter from my London friend was forwarded. She asked me to bring, without fail, the 'Corot' on Tuesday, not later than five o'clock, stating that it was to be taken to America on the boat sailing from Southampton that night.

"That was on Saturday. My first impulse was to send another line to Williams telling him to expect me back. On reflection, however, I foresaw difficulties. This sudden change in my plans might, in some way, arouse suspicion. Then, too, the committee was meeting on that Tuesday, and I was not anxious for them to surmise why, if I had returned, I could not be present during the whole of their meeting. Then, I suppose, I was too clever. For, suddenly, there dawned upon me the idea that this was an excellent chance for removing the 'Corot' while I was, apparently, abroad in Geneva. If, on some subsequent occasion, anything happened to hint that I was mixed up with the sale of this world-known picture, I could give a valuable alibi. Again, the very fact that the committee was meeting that Tuesday gave me the only opportunity I had for getting into my rooms unobserved – for, as you very soon found out, the only key was in possession of Williams. But the door would be unlocked during the luncheon hour, and the rooms would be empty. A very few minutes would suffice to remove the 'Corot.'

"I took the train to Paris the next morning, stayed the night there, and went on to London the next day, arriving there on Monday evening. I had – in case of emergencies – my very simple disguise with me, and put on hat, collar and specs in the lavatory just before the train arrived in London. I spent the night in an hotel, giving another name, and, the following morning, ran down to Exbridge, arriving there shortly after one o'clock – and made straight for St. Oswald's College. As I crossed the street towards the gate a man I knew slightly was coming out, but, like several other acquaintances I had met when coming from the station, he did not recognise me. The porter was not in his lodge as I went in. No one saw me do so.

"The surprise came, as you may imagine, when I found Hatton in what I had supposed would be an empty room, and not only that, but when I saw several of my books out of the case, the panel dropped and the cavity behind open, and Hatton in the act of just finishing unrolling the 'Corot,' while two other articles, a Cosway miniature and a jewelled Tudor dagger, said to have been the property of Sir Walter Raleigh, were lying on the table.

"I was so taken aback, that, instead of making a quick retreat as I ought to have done, I came forward into the room, uttering a hasty ejaculation. Whether it was that Hatton recognised my voice, or whether he already knew of my disguise, I shall never know, but he greeted me quite coolly – though he, too, must have been astonished at my unexpected appearance.

"'It's no use, Henlow,' he said. 'The game's up. I guessed the truth days ago.'

"I will not trouble you with our interview at length. In the course of it he explained, with the somewhat icy precision which characterised him, how he had set to work to solve the problem of that missing Cosway, how an inadvertent glance at my pocket diary, which I laid open on the table at which I was sitting side by side with him at the previous committee meeting, had given him a clue. (I was foolish enough to have jotted down one of the combinations in a letter lock in which I was interested.) How he had slowly, but ruthlessly, gathered information, and how he had taken the opportunity that day of proving the truth of his theory.

"I don't think I meant to do him any harm – in fact, I'm sure I had no such thoughts at first. But his uncalled-for interference in a matter that was no concern of his, his blank refusal to keep this matter to himself or to give me a chance to escape, his calmly uttered threat to follow me out of the room if I made a move to go, and to denounce me as a thief to the first person we met, his unshakeable determination to have justice executed on one with whom he had been friendly for years, raised the very devil in me – especially as I was driven into a corner and could see no other means to save myself. Exasperated to the full by his stubborn demeanour and threats I became blind with rage. I snatched the dagger from the table, drew it from its sheath and – well – before almost I knew what I was doing, he had fallen on the floor. I killed him!

"I suppose I ought to have been horrified. I was not. I never felt more cool in my life than when I had stabbed him. I never knew my senses more acute. Sobered, indeed, I was. All rage – and even the resentment which had caused the rage – seemed to fly on the instant. I candidly confess I was only concerned with my own safety.

"I looked at my watch. I must have been with him for nearly half an hour, for it was six minutes to two. I had another half-hour – much more time than I needed – to hide my traces and get away. I rolled up the 'Corot' ready to take with me, put the miniature and the dagger (the hilt of which I wiped first with my handkerchief to erase possible finger-prints) back in the hiding hole, and replaced the books.

"The idea suddenly struck me that someone might come in before half-past two. Williams, sometimes, looked in to see if the fire was all right. And, though I had plenty of time, I didn't want the discovery to be made till the last possible moment. I had missed the express I had intended to take back to London, but there was a stopping train at 2.20 which I could just catch, and I wanted to be in that train before Hatton was found dead. That is why I placed him in that chair and spread a newspaper I had bought the night before in London and which happened to be in my pocket, over him. Anyone coming and looking in would naturally imagine that he was either asleep or reading. Then I looked carefully round the room to see if I had left any trace of my visit, opened the door and went out.

"I had already gone down three or four of the stairs when I stopped short. I had caught a glimpse of two workmen at the bottom. Very carefully I went up again, out of view. I did not care to be seen actually coming from my rooms by anyone. I might have slipped past the porter at the gate, and, even if he had seen me, he would not have known whence I came. But I felt I dare not take this risk. What was I to do? I couldn't go back into my rooms and wait there. I should be found. The only thing I could think of was a temporary hiding place, and I did not stop at the moment to consider the possibility of that hiding place being searched when the alarm was given. On my bunch of keys was one belonging to the lock of the door of the room across the landing. I went in, and locked the door on the inside, and waited, trying to think of some means of escape.

"It was when I heard footsteps coming up the stairs that I realised that I had deliberately put myself into a trap. Far better to have passed the gauntlet of those two workmen, and to have chanced it!

"Well, there I was, my ear glued to the door. I heard the alarm! I heard the arrival of the police and the doctor. I could also hear, when the door opposite was open (as it seemed to be most of the time) scraps of conversation coming from across the landing.

"I waited – in trepidation, expecting every moment to be discovered. The minutes flew by. The members of the committee began to leave – I was still listening. Finally I gathered that only two were left – one of them a policeman, the other the college porter. I recognised his voice.

"It was those two who, unwittingly, gave me the idea. I heard the porter ask the police officer if he had looked in the wardrobe in my bedroom, and the reply that he had done so, finding only some clothes there. Then they both came on to the landing, and I held my breath. There was only a thin door between me and the gallows! The police officer questioned the porter about the room I was in, telling him to go and get the key from Williams. Then they both went down the staircase.

"Here was my chance. I came out of the room, locking the door behind me, slipped across the way, and got into the wardrobe that had been searched already. Not that I felt secure. The door into the sitting-room was open. The police officer, evidently with another, returned – Williams with them. I thought they would never leave off asking him questions. But there was more to come. After Williams had gone out those two policemen discussed the case for what must have been nearly an hour. I heard every word they said. Once one of them came into the bedroom, and I thought my time was up at last. But he did not open that wardrobe again.

"I waited an age before I finally ventured out of my hiding place. I found myself locked in my room, and, of course, I had no key. I confess I was thankful the body had been removed – I had heard them doing this. The first thing I did was to put the 'Corot' back behind the bookcase. I knew it was no use now to try to take it up to London – the boat was sailing to New York that night.

"Then I did what afterwards turned out to be a very foolish thing. I was wearing a favourite pair of shoes, and I noticed the lace of one of them was broken, so I replaced it with one which I took from a shoe in the wardrobe, throwing the broken bit I had removed on the floor of the cupboard.

"The hours passed very slowly, especially when darkness set in. And as I had not had anything since breakfast I began to be hungry. I dared not, of course, turn on the electric light. Once I struck a match to look at my watch, shutting myself in the wardrobe to do it, so that no glimmer of light could be seen through a window. I have often wondered since if that astute detective of yours got hold of that half-burnt match, which I dropped on the floor of the wardrobe, and deduced anything from it, for it was not an ordinary one. It came out of a paper packet I got at Evian-les-Bains, and had some wording on it. After my return I looked in the wardrobe to see if it was there, but, with the broken bit of lace, it had vanished, and I dared not draw attention to it by asking Williams if he had removed them.

"It was well after two in the morning that I ventured to make a move. Fortunately for me it was a pitch-black night, and the High Street was deserted. It was quite easy to let myself drop on to the pavement, creeping through the oriel window, closing it from outside, and hanging by my hands from the sill. I will not enlarge on the details of how I walked through familiar by-streets, got out into the open country, or the means by which I ultimately reached London, but you can remind your superintendent that when he called on me just after my return, and asked me if I knew of any means of escaping from my rooms, I told him it was possible to do so by dropping out of that window. I did so deliberately, with the thought in my mind that if ever the slightest suspicion should be directed against myself the police would hardly pursue it in the face of the fact that I had drawn their attention to a means of eluding them.

"And now I come to my final escape. I had come to imagine that I had eluded all danger. From my interview with your superintendent and with yourself it was easy to see that any suspicions which you had were not directed towards myself. Neither of you had, apparently, questioned the assumption that I was in Switzerland at the time of Hatton's death. I grew bold enough to transact another piece of business embracing a journey to London. The next morning

Williams brought your young detective-sergeant into the college library to see me. Directly he gave his name I remembered you had told me he was an extremely smart fellow, and I felt I should have to be careful. But, over and above this, I recognised him as a man who had been seated opposite to me in the train when I had journeyed to London, in my disguise, the day before.

"I can see now that, in the interview which followed in my rooms we were really fencing with one another. At the time his questions struck me as irrelevant, and I was secretly asking myself whether he had recognised me as his fellow-traveller. After he had gone it occurred to me to ask Williams whether your sergeant had been questioning him about my movements the day before previous to his bringing him into the library. He had not, but what Williams did tell me set me thinking. Your young officer had been asking him about that missing shoelace. It was while I was trying to puzzle it out, seated in my chair, that I happened to glance down at my shoes, and then I suddenly realised what a fool I had been to go on wearing what, as I have said, was my favourite pair, with those two odd laces in them. I felt instinctively that your police-sergeant had grasped the truth. The fact that he had asked Williams about those laces, but had never mentioned them to me, convinced me that he knew.

"I had, for a long time, prepared for the emergency in case suspicion fell on me, and I kept a sum in cash in my rooms – to say nothing of other preparations.

"I saw that it was time to be off and I did not hesitate for a moment. I went to the lodge and telephoned for a taxi.

You know the rest – up to a point. I saw your taxi come up, turn, and follow me to the station. I had my penny in readiness to get a platform ticket, for I saw that, even if I got away in the train, I should be arrested at the other end. I dashed down the subway steps and got out of the station at the other side. So far, I believe, your officers traced me soon afterwards, but what they did not discover was the fact that a bus bound for Derringford was coming along the street just as I emerged from the station. I took it – from Derringford I managed to get away to – well – as I have told you – 'somewhere in the world.'

"Those are the facts. My career is ruined, of course, and I am not without deep regret for the cause of its ruin – more especially for having taken a human life. But I have not written to you for the purpose of giving you an analysis of my conscience. We shall, I sincerely hope, never meet again. I congratulate you, however, on the efficiency of your detective officer; and, though I presume it would be useless to ask you to convey what are my heartfelt regrets to Miss Hatton – regrets which will burden me for the rest of my life, perhaps you will deem it no hypocritical sentiment on my part if I beg you, as one of the friends I had at Exbridge, though you judge me as I deserve to be judged, at least to pray for me.

"Yours,

"SIDNEY HENLOW."

We hope you enjoyed
Murder at the College

Please turn the page to read the first chapter of
Fatality in Fleet Street
by Christopher St John Sprigg

FATALITY IN
FLEET STREET

Christopher St John Sprigg

OREON

A Prime Minister Threatens

"THREE HUNDRED YEARS AGO, Lord Carpenter, I'd have had your head on a spike on Tower Hill," said the Prime Minister, the Right Hon. Claude Sanger.

Lord Carpenter made no answer beyond caressing his threatened neck reflectively.

"As it is I can only appeal to your better nature." The Prime Minister's voice faltered with the oratorical trick the wireless had made familiar to millions. Now, however, the trick was submerged in a note of genuine sincerity. "Do you realize what War means?"

Lord Carpenter, Governing Director of Affiliated Publications, the biggest newspaper group in the world, gazed thoughtfully out of the window. He saw London's roofs tossing in a troubled sea below the lemon yellow and gilt heights of the *Mercury's* gaudy building. He saw the sun glitter upon the transparent lattice-work of the Crystal Palace. But he was interested in none of these things. Force of habit made him turn his profile to his visitor, in order to exhibit his famous Napoleonesque profile with the wandering lock of hair on the high brow. Affiliated Publications' 36,563,271 readers had often scanned it admiringly in photographic form. The Right Hon. Claude Sanger now scanned it anxiously for any sign of a chink in the other's armour.

"I realize – better than you, perhaps, Sanger," answered Carpenter.

"You do not realize – you cannot realize!" The Premier's voice rolled thunderingly and his ragged features were a mask of tragedy. "Think of the holocaust of young lives! The incessant jettisoning of our accumulated savings in the bottomless sea of destruction! Remember our widows! Our sucklings instructed in the lore of hate! Our nation's veins drained of their vigour! Whatever hydra Russian Communism may be, it cannot justify this loosing of a ghastly scourge on England and the Empire. Carpenter, at this moment you are answerable to God and the innumerable posterity of our race!"

"Your oratory is as admirable as ever," answered Carpenter coldly. "I think, however, hard facts are all that matter at the moment. In the autumn of 1937, twelve months ago almost to a day, I decided that Russia must be crushed." Lighting a cigar, Carpenter mentioned his decision with the same casual air as if it had been to have his house spring-cleaned. "The deciding factor was, of course, Russia's first genuinely favourable trade balance with an unpegged exchange. That made her, for the first time, a real menace to the established order of things." With the keen enjoyment of an enthusiast explaining his hobby, Carpenter produced a map from his desk. "I determined that this country, striking up through India, should be the executioner. The clash must come sooner or later, but obviously the time for it to come is when we are strong and Russia militarily negligible. I don't propose to justify myself. I am perfectly happy in my own mind about the rightness of my aim. Therefore for the last twelve months the unique power of my papers – I think I can call it unique without boasting – has been devoted to the end I proposed—"

The Premier exploded. "By every device of dishonest propaganda! By the employment of the world's carrion crows as *agents provocateurs*! By methods which are an outrage on the fair name of Journalism!"

Carpenter raised a deprecating hand. "By the very methods which, employed in the services of the Produce More British Goods Campaign, induced you to recommend me for a Viscounty. The methods, in any case, are beside the point. They have resulted in an upheaval of popular opinion which you have as much chance of controlling as of stopping the Flying Scotsman with one hand. The Empire is simmering. It needs only one more puff of flame to make it boil over."

The Premier, arms folded, sagged slowly forward in his chair. He was a poor listener. He had reached his present position largely because he never bothered to grasp what his opponents were saying. The fact that his speeches contained no reference to their arguments gave the public the impression that they were not worth answering. This made him a tower of strength in debate, but it was a handicap in private life.

Carpenter smiled. "That puff of flame has come." He stabbed Russia in Asia with one long forefinger. "Just around here, in an obscure Soviet, an incident has occurred which, handled as it will be handled by my papers, will bring the Empire to the boil. The Foreign Office knows nothing of it. Fleet Street knows nothing of it. But I know, and tomorrow the whole Empire will know, know of it in such a way, that war will be inevitable. The Government that attempts to compromise, even your own Federated Progressive Government, will fall in a night."

Sanger was silent. He rose heavily to his feet.

"Jove, the old boy looks old," thought Jerningham, Carpenter's confidential secretary, as he brought in the Premier's hat and stick. The silence might have seemed profound with the fate of

3

nations, but the words of farewell were formal. Yet at the door the Premier paused.

"I am going back to decide whether to resign or to try to guide the ship through the coming storm," he said wearily. "Probably I shall resign. I'm getting on now, you know. Meanwhile I must warn you that if I can think of any means, lawful or unlawful, to upset your plans, I should take them without a moment's hesitation."

And for a second the elder statesman looked like the red-headed young fighter of his pre-war political apprenticeship.

Carpenter laughed with unruffled good temper. "You see we are none of us pacifists when it comes to the pinch."

— II —

"Take a note, Jerningham," said Carpenter briskly, replacing the map in the desk.

Hands in pocket, the "Chief" of the largest publishing organization in the world strode up and down the room. Suddenly he turned to Jerningham. "What the devil do you mean by wearing that foul tie in my office?" he barked, dragging the offending green object out of the opening of his secretary's impeccable lounge suit. Raised in anger, his voice lost its veneer of refinement and became grating. "You're nothing but a clerk. Remember it and dress like one, not like a Gaiety chorister."

Jerningham flushed. His handsome but weak face twisted with an expression which might have been shame or fury. His hand shook as he replaced the tie. "I beg your pardon, sir," he answered meekly.

Carpenter resumed his pacing. At last he spoke, with the colourless precision of a dictating machine.

"This is to be the main leader page article. It must run to four columns with a streamer headline. The first two paragraphs are to be in bold type. The article should be illustrated by a photo of myself, of Stalin – the most repulsive one in our files – and that photo of crowds lying down flat on their faces in a Moscow street during the Tsarist succession riots – only give it the caption 'Religious procession mowed down by Bolshevist soldiers.' We've used it before, about a year ago. Now begin. 'We must fight or go under! The Brezka Atrocity is the final move in the Bolshevist policy of encirclement stop The object of that policy is the obliteration of the Empire comma the only bulwark between Communism and Civilization stop' That last sentence to be in small caps..."

He halted a moment and spoke down the dictograph. "Hubbard? Bring up all we've got about the Brezka concession at once."

Then in a monotonous voice he continued. The tone was dreary, but the article was one which, like all the Chief's writing, would go straight home to the bosom of the average man, of which Carpenter himself was a glorified enlargement.

"Rotten, Hubbard, rotten," shouted Carpenter, glancing through the meagre file of cuttings brought to him by Hubbard. "Much more than this has appeared! You get more damned inefficient every day."

Hubbard gave a strangled cry of protest. The mildest of men, this was enough to stir him to bitterness. Jerningham felt a fellow feeling for him, smarting in his turn under the Chief's rough tongue. Jerningham knew Hubbard's reputation on Fleet Street. A wizened, parchment-faced old man, he dwelt from year's end to year's end in the dusty library of the *Mercury*. He had never been known to take a holiday or be away ill. Some said he was expiating the terrible day when he gave a reporter, told to write up the obituary of a politician called Armstrong, the *dossier* of a novelist of the same name, whose obituary had accordingly appeared the next morning. Since that morning, it was credibly asserted, he had never been seen to smile again. His perpetual residence in the library was, however, of some value. The filing system he adopted for newspaper cuttings was so elaborate that it was believed no one but himself could grasp it. Imagination quavered at the prospect of his death. But the system was worked by him with astounding speed. He boasted that anything that had appeared about anything could be produced by him in two minutes.

Now, in his agitation, his shaking hand spilled snuff all over his jacket. He brushed his lapels and nervously tapped down the lid.

"Damn it," roared the Chief, "I will not have that disgusting habit here. Jerningham, mop up that stuff from the floor!"

Blinking up at him, the librarian insisted on making his protest. "I am quite certain nothing has appeared which is not in that folder," he asserted.

"Nonsense, nonsense," said the other angrily. "I'll have to get a filing expert in to teach you some lessons, or better still, boot you out altogether."

Even Jerningham was staggered at this outrageous threat, but Hubbard said nothing. His beady eyes regarded the Chief coldly behind his pebble eyeglasses.

"All right," Carpenter said at last, "you can go."

The Chief did not go on with the dictation of his article immediately. Hubbard had gone. He stared ahead reflectively. "Extraordinary that such an unprepossessing fellow should have such a charming daughter," he said reflectively. "When I first saw her in the Advertisement Canvassing Department and asked her name, I could hardly believe it. What a figure!"

Jerningham, kneeling on the floor wielding a duster, thanked his stars that at least he hadn't a daughter working in the office of whom Carpenter spoke in that tone, and knowledge of Carpenter's weakness was by no means confined to his secretary. Very unwise of Hubbard, thought Jerningham, for even he must know by this time how things stood between Carpenter and his daughter.

— III —

The thinkers of England's thoughts sat round in the draughty Board Room at the top of the lemon yellow *Mercury* building which dominated Fleet Street.

In other words, there was a Special General Conference of the *Mercury* called by Lord Carpenter. The "General" in the title accounted for the wide assortment of people who were present, from Editor to the Publisher. The "Special" in the title accounted for the equally notable omissions in the ranks. On the whole, however, the band was sufficiently representative of the hard-working souls who formed the conversation and conscience of democratic England.

At the moment they all looked a little uneasy, except Grovermuller, the Editor. A dapper, silver-haired, bird-like little man immersed in a ponderous-looking review, he sat in the centre of the crescent of chairs. The hierarchy of the paper dwindled in orderly formation to the tips of the crescent, and at the extreme right hand tip was Charles Venables, late society editor, but now crime expert of the *Mercury*. There was a faint air of surprise even on his innocuous face as he toyed with his monocle, and seeing it his neighbour, Perry, the Art Editor, endeavoured to reassure him.

"It's all right. This is a Gathering of the Good Boys."

This mysterious phrase was not lost on Charles. The last gathering had been a Gathering of the Bad Boys – those members of the Advertising Staff whom Carpenter had considered responsible for a dwindling in the *Mercury's* revenue. Carpenter, mottled with rage, had screamed invective for half an hour at his shaken staff. He had wound up by stating that Sergeant Capes, the commissionaire, was a better Advertisement Manager than any of them, and had installed the bewildered worthy in the Manager's office at the Manager's salary until such time as the revenue was restored to its old figure. Meanwhile, the Manager received Sergeant Capes's salary. The Advertising Staff agreed to leave in a body that evening. The next morning calmer counsels prevailed, and the succeeding issue grossed a revenue five percent above the average. That evening Sergeant Capes, gloriously drunk, was thrown out of the Savoy Grill Room, after sweeping Sir David Lowder, the famous advertising magnate, into an alcoholic embrace of kinship. On the second morning all was quiet.

But this was a Gathering of the Good Boys. Charles's neighbour, Perry, for instance, was the only Art Editor in Fleet Street, in fact probably in the world, who made up the picture page in a morning-coat and spats, instead of the waistcoat and dusty trousers more usual to the tribe. Perry's languid accent matched his appearance, both of which were deceptive. In his time, as a stripling press photographer, Perry had been towed by a submarine on an aquaplane in the North Sea, hung by his legs from an aeroplane undercarriage in mid-air, lain on his belly along the smoking-hot bonnet of a Grand Prix racer cornering at 90 m.p.h., all to obtain shots a little more distinctive than those of his competitors. And he had the knack of inspiring his cameramen to go and do likewise.

"What is the Chief's allocution going to be about?" asked Venables, feeling rather like a member of a Fourth Form summoned *en masse* before the Head. Even the nickname the "Chief" was like a schoolboy tradition.

Through the ramifications of Affiliated Publications Limited, whose journals accounted for eighty-five percent of the country's circulations registered at the Audit Bureau, Carpenter now wielded a power in the newspaper world of imperial dimensions. But he still loved to remind Fleet Street in the mellow, paternal tones he had acquired with the passing years, that he was, after all, a "working journalist." Nothing pleased him more than that his staff should visualize his active shirt-sleeved co-operation with them, such as was suggested by that nickname, the "Chief".

"Anything might happen, old boy," admitted Perry. "The Chief may burst into tears and say he has remembered us all in his will. He did that last time. Or he may walk in as he did once, look round in dead silence, mutter, 'Magnificent! Magnificent!' and walk out again. We may all be given a rousing speech and told to look in our pay envelopes next week, and when we look, find the same as usual. That happened once, you know."

This not being helpful, Charles endeavoured to find enlightenment by scanning the thirty-odd men – and women – decorating the office. They did not look at their ease – but it was not an office conducive to ease. Opposite the crescent of chairs was a full-length Orpen of the Chief. Round the walls were hung the remarkable collection of weapons gathered by the Chief in his wanderings. The furniture was massive – blackened oak, burgeoning and heaving with baroque carving. The carpet was inch-deep with pile. The Chief was just going through a period of craving for luxury – a reaction, perhaps, from the year before, when a longing for austerity had stripped his office of all superfluous furniture. The unfortunate results of this craving instantly depressed any visitor on entry to the room, even in the most auspicious circumstances.

In any case, being one of the Chief's Good Boys was, strangely enough, more depressing than to be a Bad one. He that is down need fear no fall. The whole staff of the *Mercury*, from the

Advertisement Manager to the Messenger Boy, Art Perkins No. 25, were, as it were, distributed on two ladders, those on the right ascending in the Chief's favour, those on the left descending. Only the Editor, Eric Grovermuller, by some uncanny gift, was able to remain perpetually at the top, teetering dangerously at times, but always recovering himself by his supreme talent for poise.

Now all of the staff gathered together in that office were near the top of the ladder. Venables had just sensationally solved the Garden Hotel Mystery. Perry had obtained an exclusive photo of the *Macon's* forced descent on the South Pole by a brilliantly improvised organization of speed-boats, dog-sleighs, and aeroplanes. And all being near the top of the ladder, all feared the inevitable approach of the return to the abyss.

"It is the Russian business, of course," boomed out Andrews' voice suddenly from Perry's elbow. Andrews, enormous and shaggy, carried heartiness to an extreme which might have made the judicious suspicious. With reason – Andrews was the shrewdest City Editor in England. More than one famous swindler, expounding his schemes with invincible assurance to this cheery soul, had suddenly felt deflated by a cruel thrust at the weak spot in his scheme, delivered with the utmost *bonhomie*. And the point was subsequently pressed in the City column with a persistence which was attributed to malice. Quite wrongly, because Andrews did not know what malice was.

"You, my lads," he went on, "have the privilege of seeing how patriotism is manufactured, and war made. In twenty years' time your memoirs will be history. Meanwhile, you will probably have been blown to bits, and, anyway, you will not be believed."

"I suppose it's rather a dirty job we're doing," mused Venables. "But a fascinating kind of dirt..."

"Here," interrupted Perry, "is the Chief."

Follow the story by reading
Fatality in Fleet Street
by Christopher St John Sprigg
ISBN 9781909349759

available from all book shops or direct:

See further Golden Age titles overleaf:

Why not sign up to our infrequent Newsletter to be told of our latest titles before anyone else?

oleanderpress.com/golden-age-crime

OREON titles in this series

The Essex Murders
by Vernon Loder
ISBN 9781915475053

The Boat Race Murder
by R. E. Swartwout
ISBN 9781915475039

Please choose: USA   UK

Murder at the College
by Victor L. Whitechurch
ISBN 9781999900489

The Charing Cross Mystery
by J.S. Fletcher
ISBN 9781909349711

The Doctor of Pimlico
by William Le Queux
ISBN 9781909349735

Who Killed Alfred Snowe?
by J. S. Fletcher
ISBN 9781915475015

The Yorkshire Moorland Mystery
by J. S. Fletcher
ISBN 9781915475008

Fatality in Fleet Street
by Christopher St John Sprigg
ISBN 9781909349759

Made in United States
Orlando, FL
24 December 2022

27651432R00162